D1527604

LYING IN THE WEEDS

FRANK SHIMA

This book is a work of fiction. Names, characters, places, and incidents are products of the author's imagination or are used fictitiously. Any resemblance to actual events or persons, living or dead, is entirely coincidental.

Copyright © 2023 by Frank Shima

All rights reserved.

DEDICATION

This book is dedicated to my wife,
Robin, who has helped and supported
my writing over the years, and to
Franny Tuma, my number one fan!

TABLE OF CONTENTS

PART ONE: THE FIND - 1963

PART TWO: THE JOURNAL - 1875

PART THREE: THE SOLUTION - 1963

PART FOUR: JEZEBEL – 1962

PART FIVE: JANA - 1876

PART ONE: THE FIND - 1963

CHAPTER 1

A WHALE IN THE CORNFIELD

It was a day like any other when we found it. I knew right away nothing good would come from it. I was right.

It happened on a day when I was doing nothing. Sometimes doing nothing is good, but saying you're doing nothing might turn out bad. This occurred one day as I was playing in the barn when I was thirteen years old.

"What you doing, Jimmie?" my grandfather asked.

"Nothing."

"You want to go for a ride?"

"Yes!"

The answer to that was always yes. A ride kept you from doing some chores on the farm. Or from sitting around being bored. It could be a ride to the feed mill to grind feed. Or a ride to the lake to catch fish. Sometimes a ride meant following a truck hauling sweet corn to the Green Giant canning factory. Ears of corn would fall off and be left behind to be picked up by us as we followed.

Whenever I rode with Uncle John, he always seemed to get a flat tire. He would look at the tire and say *Sakra Menske*. It wasn't until I was seven that I learned that *Sakra Menske* were swear words and not Czech for a flat tire.

School had just ended for the year. My job now was to help Uncle John plant oats and corn. It was late in the year, but an unusually wet spring kept him from getting into this field. My dad had driven me out to help him. I brought my dog, Shep, along too. Uncle John wasn't paying me anything, and he was going to get his money's worth.

When I left the barn, I saw that the answer should have been no this time. Outside stood my frail, skinny grandfather in his seventies who had come out to help Uncle John. He and his number one farm horse, Jeden, waited in the yard. Jeden because that is the Czech word for one. My smile changed to a frown when I saw the stone boat or *lod'* hitched to Jeden. The stone boat was a heavy sled made out of three-inch oak planks, with the front of the planks angled upward. My grandfather used it to clear the ground of huge rocks that had grown in the fields over the winter. I think it was his favorite thing to do. I guess there wasn't much else for him to do on a farm in the 1960s.

As much as my grandfather pretended he didn't like kids, I could tell he did. Maybe not as much as his horse, Jeden, and picking rocks, but more than he let on.

My job for the day would be to walk alongside the stone boat and pick up any rocks that were bigger than a baseball. If I missed anything larger, it was sure to break some piece of farm equipment. According to my dad, rocks were the only thing that would grow on this farm.

A giant boulder that was impossible to remove lived in the middle of the cornfield. Only the top part of the rock stuck out of the dirt, much like an iceberg in the ocean. Uncle John called it the whale, and he just worked around it.

I walked on one side of the stone boat, and my grandfather took the other. He carried a huge pry bar to dig the stubborn rocks out of the ground.

When my grandfather wanted to move ahead, he clicked his tongue twice, and Jeden pulled forward. When he wanted to stop, he again clicked his tongue twice, and Jeden stopped. So I figured two clicks meant either stop or go. A tractor couldn't do that.

I clicked my tongue twice. Jeden didn't move a muscle.

When I asked why, my grandfather said, "He only listens to me."

Jeden was one smart horse.

Filling the sled was only half the job. It had to be unloaded at the rock pile next to the pasture when it could hold no more rocks. At least I could ride back and forth.

Late in the afternoon, when we were on the far end of the field, I reached down to pick up a football-sized rock. When I saw what it was, I stopped and stared at it.

"Come on, Jimmie. The rocks aren't going to pick themselves up."

I thought it would be better for me if they did.

"Hurry and pick that up, why don't you?"

I couldn't move. My grandfather finally turned toward me. "Do I have to do that myself then?"

"No. Look."

I saw that what appeared to be a rock was actually a human skull.

"What do we do, Gramps?"

My grandfather didn't answer; he walked over to me. He was bent forward at the hip, probably from too many years of picking rocks. He elbowed me aside and picked up the skull. He held the skull much like one would hold a bowling ball and threw it underhand into the tall weeds in the ditch.

CHAPTER 2

WHAT SKULL?

Darkness forced us to end my grandfather's fun for the day. There were enough rocks in those fields to make him happy for the rest of his life and make me unhappy for the rest of mine. No matter how many stones we removed each year, others had cropped up to take their place. I even wondered whether the rocks we had picked before moved back to their homes in the fields when we weren't looking.

I looked up at my grandfather, who walked alongside Jeden. He didn't need to guide his horse back to the barn. Jeden knew his way home from his years toiling on the farm.

"What about that skull?" I asked.

"What skull?"

"The one we found in the field. The one you tossed in the weeds."

"Too much sun. That's what you got today. Makes you see things that aren't there."

"It was there. I'm sure it was."

"What would a skull be doing there? It's a cornfield, not a graveyard."

With that, we arrived at the barnyard and the end of the discussion. Jeden stopped beside the machine shed where my grandfather stored the stone boat. I helped my grandfather unhitch the stone boat and remove

Jeden's bridle, harness, and reins. Without a word, Jeden walked into the barn and entered his stall. He knew his workday was done. He was lucky. I still had my evening chores to do.

That night I couldn't sleep. All I could think of was that skull. Maybe my grandfather could forget about it, but I couldn't. Whose skull was it? How did it get into our field? How long had it been there? Should we have contacted the sheriff?

I thought of asking my dad about it. I wondered if he would believe me. I was starting not to believe me.

Then I remembered something else about the skull. It looked like there was a hole in the middle of the forehead! Was it a bullet hole? It had to be.

The following day, I got up before anyone else. I had never done that before. It was almost impossible to do since Uncle John got up before the sun. I ran out to the ditch.

The sun appeared on the horizon to the east when I reached the spot where my grandfather had tossed the skull. I searched through the weeds, and all I could find was nothing.

I thought I might be wrong about the exact spot, so I looked in each direction. I did find something. A lot of somethings. A rusted-out Hamm's beer can. An old boot without a sole, but new shoelaces, which I considered strange. Underwear, women's underwear, I think, which I dropped immediately. A weathered, unopened letter addressed to our neighbor, which I would toss into her mailbox later. A shiny, new quarter. My morning wouldn't be a complete waste.

I continued to search through the weeds for an hour, and I couldn't find the skull. The skull was gone!

CHAPTER 3

SNOOPY

I had to find out about the skull. I could ask my grandfather again. He would probably tell me that it didn't exist. I knew the person I had to ask.

I found Uncle John in the barn finishing up the morning milking. Ruddy-faced and stout, he was dressed in patched work clothes and boots he'd worn more years than I'd known him. He was sitting on a stool milking Number Four by hand. He didn't give cows names, just numbers.

"Uncle John?"

"What's up, Jimmie?"

"Yesterday, when I picked up rocks with Gramps, I…"

"Did you find any?" he interrupted.

"About ten loads full."

"Then I won't be hitting any rocks when I disk today."

"I guess. I found something else."

"Yeah. Like what?"

"I found a skull."

"Are you sure? What would that be doing out there? Let me see it."

"That's just it. It's gone. Gramps threw it into the ditch, and now it's not there."

He got up and pulled the pail full of milk from under the cow. "What did Gramps say about it?"

"That we didn't find any skull."

"Then you probably didn't. I wouldn't worry about it."

"I *am* worrying about it. I thought of different stories of how it got there. It belonged to a bank robber who was shot while trying to escape. Or a hunter who was accidentally shot during deer hunting season. Or even someone who had taken his life in the middle of our field. How long had it been there? Why hadn't it been found before? How many years would it last if it had been buried in our field?"

"Slow down, Jimmie. Slow down. What else did you find where you found the skull? Any other bones? Any identification buried with it?"

"Other bones? Identification? I didn't think of that. I've got to go."

I took Shep and searched through the weeds in the ditch again. Even with Shep's help, I couldn't find the skull. Next, I walked to where I had discovered it. I couldn't place the exact spot. I walked back and forth in an area about the size of a baseball infield. Shep looked too, but I don't think she knew what we were looking for. We found nothing. Just more rocks.

"What're you doing?"

I turned to see a kid younger than me, skinny, a little shorter, with bright red hair.

"Who are you? You scared the hell out of me!"

"I'm your new neighbor."

"Oh, hi. What's your name?"

"We just moved in next door a few weeks ago."

He didn't tell me his name. I decided I would call him Red.

"Uncle John didn't say anyone moved in."

"It was in the middle of the night. Plus, we don't have much stuff."

"It's a strange time to be moving."

"Not for us."

Red walked to the area where Shep and I had searched. "I figured you were looking for rocks. You did that yesterday. So what are you looking for here?"

I decided I should maybe call him Snoopy instead of Red. I wasn't going to tell him about the skull.

Instead, I came up with another story. "I dropped a jackknife here yesterday. I was hoping I might be able to find it."

"A jackknife. Are you sure?"

"I ought to know if I lost a jackknife. Shouldn't I?"

"If you say so. It's a mighty big field. I'm not doing anything. I could help you look for it."

Great. He was going to help me find a knife that didn't exist. However, I couldn't tell him not to help. We searched for ten minutes. Shep and I were the only ones searching. Snoopy sort of stood around, chuckling to himself.

I stopped searching and glared at Snoopy. "You're not much help."

"I could help you from now until hell freezes over, but we won't find anything."

"How do you know?"

"Because you never lost a jackknife, and you never found a skull like you think you did."

"Not you too, Snoopy. I know I found a skull yesterday."

His nickname didn't seem to bother him. "No. You think you found one. You didn't. Not a real one anyway."

"Sure. Gramps threw it away."

"That was just a fake skull I stole from a science class."

"You mean, you hid the skull in the field?"

"Sure. I had to bury it four times between your trips unloading the rocks before you finally found it. Then I dug it out of the ditch last night."

"And that's why I couldn't find it in the weeds."

"Nice trick, huh?"

"Come on, Shep. Let's go home."

I turned and marched across the field toward our house. The sound of his laughter faded away, but I could still hear it in my mind.

It was going to be a long summer.

CHAPTER 4

A HOLE IN THE WALL

How could a fake skull have fooled me? It was worse than a few years ago when another neighbor kid pretended to be Superman. I had fallen for that too.

In fact, the more I thought about it, the more I wondered whether I had been fooled. Was the skull fake? It seemed real, not made of plastic like those in a science class. Plus, it looked like it had been buried in the earth for a long time, not placed there for me to find. If Snoopy did hide it, he went through a lot of work for a stupid prank.

I decided to continue my search for more bones. Shep searched too, for about five minutes. Then she headed toward the pasture. She wasn't running like she was chasing a rabbit or anything, but she walked with her nose to the ground as if following a scent. Shep was on to something. Maybe she was on the scent of the skull. I followed her to find out what it was.

We crossed the fence and over the alfalfa field toward the pasture. She jumped over another fence which I crawled under. I followed her through the woods. She snaked her way around trees and brush, which I had a more difficult time with.

We finally came to a part of the pasture I hadn't bothered exploring. Shep ran into a gully with me trailing the distance of about home to first base. Then she disappeared. One second, she was there. The next second, she was gone. I ran to the spot where I had last seen her, along the far side of the gully.

"Shep! Where are you?"

There was no answer. I searched through the brush and weeds. There was no sign of her. I should have named her Houdini.

"Shep!" I called again.

This time I heard something. It was Shep's bark, but it sounded far away. How could it be when she was just here? I followed the sound of her barking. Then along the side of the gully, I saw an opening. I could hear Shep barking inside. I crawled through the brush into the darkness. With no flashlight, how would I ever find her in there?

At the head of the cave, there was just enough light from outside for me to see a long rope on a pulley off to the side. Next to it, I spotted a box of candles and boxes of kitchen matches. A few steps in, I saw openings to other tunnels that branched in different directions. I would need a flashlight to investigate each of these tunnels. A guy could get lost in here.

I lit a candle and decided to follow Shep's barking. The dim light from the candle barely made a dent in the darkness of the cave. I came to a dead end. I retraced my steps. I heard Shep bark and entered another branch of the tunnel toward her. Several openings appeared on each side as I meandered through the tunnel.

Finally, I got to Shep. She was lying on a rug next to a large, old chair with a cushion on its seat. A table and two chairs sat in one corner, and a bed in the other. It appeared that at one time, someone had lived here. Books occupied a makeshift shelf in the far corner.

I sat on the chair near Shep. Dirt jumped up into the air and onto my face. I wiped it from my eyes. On the side of the chair was a small stand. Many old, weathered books were on the stand, some with Czech titles. I picked one up, opened it, and read the words handwritten on the first page, *Marek Kniha*. The other books contained the same handwriting. It looked like these books belonged to someone named Marek Kniha.

The last book on the bottom was different. It was written in English. I turned to the first page, and the word JOURNAL was written in huge capital letters.

The flame from the candle burned my fingers as the candle went out. I sat in the pitch-black darkness. I had been so intent on reading the journal that I hadn't been paying attention to the candle.

"*Sakra Menske!*"

No, it wasn't a flat tire. It was worse. I had left the box of candles at the entrance to the cave. Worse yet, I also forgot the box of matches there, so I couldn't light my way back using one of those.

I was so disoriented I couldn't remember the path that got me here. I reached down and groped for Shep. My hands found only the rug Shep was lying on. Or had been lying on. She wasn't there either.

"Shep! Shep!"

I thought I heard someone laughing from outside the cave. Then Shep answered with a few barks. Barks that I could barely hear. She was no longer in the cave. She had left without me.

I got down on my hands and knees and searched the area around the rug. I widened my search until my hands touched the side of the cave. This was getting me nowhere. I decided to get up and follow the sides of the cave to the entrance. I got to my feet and banged my head on the table under which I had crawled.

"*Sakra Menske!*"

I decided to follow the sides of the cave to the entrance. How would I know which of the branches of the cave to follow? I might never make it out.

Then I felt something rub my legs. I jumped back, wondering what sort of creature might be living here. Then I heard panting and felt a tongue lick my hand. Shep had come back to save me.

CHAPTER 5

TRAPPED AGAIN

Shep guided me to the entrance of the cave, for all the good it would do. The opening to the cave was blocked. Did Snoopy do this? I was trapped again as I had been in the bank two years ago. No one was coming at nine in the morning to get me out this time. No one knew I was there. Only Shep.

I groped around in the dark. The only things I could find were the candles and matches. I lit one of the candles and looked around.

I dropped down to my knees and grabbed one of the huge rocks blocking the exit. It wouldn't budge. I looked for something to use as a lever to pry the rock loose. It was hopeless.

Maybe there was another exit that I could use. Shep had disappeared again and was probably looking for another way out. I grabbed some matches and some candles and started to explore the cave, looking for an opening.

This time I had an idea. I picked up the end of the rope and tied it to my waist. That way, I could find my way back again.

I took the first right I came to, a branch I hadn't taken before. It seemed to go on forever, at least from what I could see in the darkness. On one side of the wall, I saw some strange markings in white paint. It could have been Czech writing. Or maybe they were just meaningless scribbles.

Then I saw a picture. I held the candle up to it. It was a painting of a cow. A deformed-looking cow, if you could call it a cow. Who would draw a picture of a cow on the side of the cave?

A little farther on, I saw paintings on another wall. This looked like a pig. Yes, it was a pig. In school, I learned that Neanderthal cavemen drew petroglyphs or art on their walls. This must be the same thing. Did ancient cavemen live in Minnesota? Why would anyone do that?

On the opposite wall, I saw a drawing of a rudimentary house. It had doors and windows and a chimney with smoke coming out of it.

This wasn't the work of a caveman. This person took some time and tried to make this place his home. Where we hung paintings on a wall, he drew pictures. Had someone been trapped in here before?

I continued onward and found another picture on the wall. This time, it looked like a horse. This whole branch of the cave was like a painting of a farmyard because up ahead, I saw a barn and some trees. Then I saw the gully. It was probably the same gully that I was in now.

Up ahead, I saw some light toward the end of this branch of the tunnel. Excitedly, I ran toward what seemed to be sunlight coming from an opening above me. The only problem was that this opening was so high I couldn't reach it.

"Shep! Shep!" I yelled.

She didn't answer. I looked, and there was no way to climb up the side of the wall. I couldn't reach this passage to my freedom which was directly above me.

Then I heard barking, and I looked up. I saw Shep looking down at me from the opening above. It was as if Shep was saying, why don't you just come right up here? At least, I think that's what she was saying.

Then next to Shep, I saw a girl. She yelled down, "Is someone down there?"

"Yeah, it's me. Jimmie."

"What are you doing?"

"I'm calling up to you."

"I mean, what are you doing down there, Jimmie? How did you get there? This dog found me and led me this way and here you are. Can you get out?"

"Uh, no. I'm trapped here."

"How did you get in there? Did you fall into this hole?"

"No," I answered. "I went through an opening on the other end."

"Why don't you just go out that opening?"

"Because someone blocked it up. I think it was some little kid with red hair."

"Oh, you mean my evil little brother. It sounds like something he'd do. He's always doing stuff like this. How can I find the other end of this cave?" she asked.

"Go down into the pasture and follow the path and you'll see a gully. Take Shep along with you. I think she'll lead you to it."

"Okay. Go back to where you got in, and I'll try to find it."

Then they disappeared. I made my way back with the help of the rope. Then I came to the blocked opening. I lit another candle since the one I had was going out. I listened for sounds outside. I didn't hear anything. Finally, I heard Shep bark, and I heard the girl from outside.

"Hello. Are you there?"

"Yes. I'm here. Can you get me out?"

"I don't know. The entrance is blocked up. I think I can get it unblocked, but it'll take a while. Freddie did an excellent job of trapping you in there. I don't know, it just seems like something he would do."

"I'll try moving some rocks and boulders from in here. Maybe, we can meet in the middle."

I heard noises from outside the cave. I dug one rock free. A tiny rock the size of a football. Eventually, I could see some light coming through one of the cracks in the opening. Soon I might be free of this dungeon. A few more rocks moved. After a few more minutes, there was an opening large enough for Shep to crawl through, which she did. She jumped into the cave and licked my face. I was never so happy to see Shep in my whole life. Eventually, there was an opening big enough for me to crawl through, which I quickly did.

When I got outside, I saw a girl. She was about an inch or so taller than me, and she also had red hair. Her hands were dirty, probably from digging out the opening to the cave. She wore dirty overalls and a dirty Farmall cap with the bill over her right ear. She wore galoshes with buckles on the sides.

She was the most beautiful girl I had ever seen.

CHAPTER 6

LUCKY ME

The girl had taken off her cap; her curly, red hair hung below her shoulders. Her blue eyes sparkled above her freckles. She looked about a year older than me, maybe because she was taller. While I had developed muscles working on the farm, I had stopped growing for some reason and was shorter than most boys my age.

"I'm lucky you showed up," I said.

"I didn't have much choice. Shep was very insistent."

"Was someone laughing out here?"

"Probably my brother. I don't know where he is now."

"Do you live around here?" I asked.

"Yeah, we just moved into the next farm over."

"At least your brother didn't lie about that."

"It'd be one of the first things he has never lied about in his whole life. He's always making up stories. If he had come to me and said you were trapped in the cave, I would never have shown up."

"I'm glad it was Shep then."

"So am I," she said.

"Do you go to school around here?"

"At the high school next fall. A sophomore. We just moved from Belle Plaine. So I don't know anyone around here."

"Of course, you've only been here just a few weeks."

"My dad's put me to work. My snotty brother too, but he's disappeared. He doesn't do much work when he is around. I'm going to end up doing it all myself. Are you going to high school too?"

I was glad she thought I was old enough to attend high school.

"At the junior high. I'm only in ninth grade."

"That means we won't be in any classes together."

My heart sank. I wanted to be in a class with her. I wanted to be in *every* class with her! What was I thinking? I had just met her. I don't know if it was love or something that seemed like it. I wanted to spend the rest of my life with her. How could that be? Why would she be interested in me?

I hope she didn't want to be a farmer. I wanted nothing to do with that. I wouldn't want to do that even if she did. Why was I worrying about that? She wouldn't be interested in me.

She asked, "Do you live on this farm?"

"I live in town now."

"Oh, that's too bad," she said.

"I'll be here a lot. I help my uncle out here on the farm during the summer. He's getting old, over sixty. I can do things and get to places in machinery he can't anymore with his fingers all gnarled up from arthritis. Whatever that is."

"That's an old people's disease. You'll be lucky if you get it because at least then, you know, you've made it to be old."

"You've got a point there. If you part your hair right."

19

She looked puzzled. "What do you mean?"

"It's just a stupid saying. If you part your hair right, you'll get a point on your head."

"I have a point on the top of my head?"

"No. You have a pretty, round head."

I couldn't believe I said that. Even though any girl would like to have a pretty, round head like hers, that's for sure.

She said, "I'd like to live in town. Maybe someday."

"I'd like that too. We have a place in town, but it isn't very nice."

"At least it's in town. Nothing ever happens on the farm."

"Something is happening here now," I said. "I can't figure out what happened to that skull."

"What skull?"

"I thought Shep was following its scent. I was looking for it when my candle went out. I only took one candle and no matches. So when my candle died, I was in the dark."

"Well, that was stupid."

"Oh yeah, you got that right. I've never felt so dumb. I take that back. I've been stupid so many times in my life that if I could add them all together, you'd think I'd learn something from it. I don't. I'd still be stupid because some people are just born this way where they do dumb things."

"That's not a dumb thing. I think you were just excited about what you found. Then there's my brother who is the mean kind of stupid."

"I'm glad I'm the happy kind."

"I'd rather have that," she said. "Say, now that we know we can get out, let's go back in and look inside and explore."

"Don't you have any chores to do?"

"Yes. But I have time. How about you?"

I said, "My chores are finished. Before I went into the cave, I was looking in the ditch for the skull."

"What would it be doing there?"

"My grandfather threw it there. I found it buried in the field while we picked rocks."

"Picked rocks?"

"You know. Rocks come up every winter, and you have to pick them up, so they don't damage the equipment when we're out in the field."

"Makes sense. About the skull. I've something to tell you before we go into the cave."

"What's that?" I asked.

"Back five years ago, when I was just a kid, my brother found a skull. It was an old skull. He used it to play tricks on people. I thought he'd gotten rid of it. I'm guessing he took the skull and buried it in your field when you weren't looking. It was just a trick. That's why you couldn't find it in the ditch. It's something he always does. You should see him on Halloween. He's got more tricks like that when we go trick or treating."

"I've never been trick or treating."

"You get a lot of free candy, but you're too old for that, Jimmie."

"I'm glad you think so."

"Freddie put it in my bed. I woke up next to a skull."

"I'm glad I don't have a brother like that."

"You can have this one if you want."

I said, "No. I have a brother older than me. He didn't pull tricks on me, but you sure didn't want him helping you. He's sort of lazy."

"Sounds like my brother."

"Then you probably wouldn't like him. Let's go in the cave."

"And see if there's another skull," she said.

"I thought you told me your brother was playing a trick."

"When I think about it, Fred isn't smart enough to play that kind of trick. He might have found it in the ditch, but I don't think he hid it among the rocks. The rocks are smarter than him. Maybe I can help find out the story behind the skull. Let's search together. Partner?"

"Partner!" I agreed.

In that case, I hoped we'd never find the skull. We would be spending a lot of time together.

CHAPTER 7

BACK FOR MORE

I no longer needed the rope because I knew which turns to take and which not to. We found ourselves in the branch with paintings on the wall.

"I wonder who'd do that," she said.

"Maybe someone lived in here, and it might have been his skull that I found."

"I think it's some artwork that whoever was in this cave used to entertain himself."

We left that branch and made our way to the room with the bed and the chairs.

"This is the room where I found the journal," I said.

"Did you see this before?"

"What?"

"Look at all these books. I've read a lot of these. Treasure Island."

"I've read that too," I said.

"I like reading about places I've never been before and imagining I was there."

"I like reading those kinds of books too, but it's hard for me to picture being on an island in the middle of an ocean. When I've never even seen an ocean."

"We have. We went to California to this park called Disneyland," she said.

"Disneyland. I think I've seen it on television."

"They have Mickey Mouse, and we went on rides. Afterward, we went out to see the Pacific Ocean. When you see the Pacific Ocean, you wouldn't believe any body of water could be so huge. It's so big you feel like you could drown just looking at it."

"By the way, what is your name?" I asked.

"I was wondering when you were going to ask. My name is Rachel."

I'd never heard such a pretty name. Of course, if her name had been Snot Rag, I would still think it was just as beautiful. Then again, maybe not.

"We should be getting back home. It must be getting late."

She said, "Yeah, I agree."

We made our way back to the exit. When we got there, she screamed.

"I don't believe it," I said.

"I believe it. He did it again. I'm going to kill him."

"Not if I kill him first."

CHAPTER 8

THE GREAT ESCAPE

Someone blocked the entrance again.

"How the hell are we going to get out of here?" she said. "No one knows we're here."

"And Shep is here with us. She can't find someone else to help us out of here. How are we going to get out?"

"Let's start digging."

I got on my hands and knees, and Rachel did as well. We clawed at the boulders, but her brother had done an even better job blocking the exit than he had last time. It was as if he had cemented all the boulders together.

"Even if we had a lever, we couldn't get out," I said.

"Okay. Now what?"

"Let's look at that other exit to the cave where I first saw you."

"It's too high," she said.

"I know. I have an idea."

I grabbed the end of the rope again.

"Why do you need that? You know the way by heart by now."

"I just need to detach the rope from the pulley and take the rope along with me."

"What are you doing?"

"Like I said. I have an idea."

We took the branch with the drawings of the cow, pig, and barn.

She said, "Maybe we should draw a dungeon in here. That's what this place is. It would be a perfect dungeon."

We got to the opening and looked up. The sky was still blue. It meant it was still daylight, and Rachel's parents wouldn't be looking for her yet. I made a loop at the end of the rope and tossed it up in the air. I remembered seeing a tree root sticking out near the top, just below the exit. If I could snag the loop on the root, it might be strong enough to hold us. We could climb up and out of here.

I tossed once and came far short. I threw it again and again and missed.

"Let me try," she said. She tossed and came even shorter. "This is getting us nowhere."

"Yeah. Let me try again," I said.

I tossed it again. After two or three more times, it finally caught and hooked onto the root.

"Now, all I have to do is climb up the rope."

She said, "I can do this. I've done it in gym class many times. We climb up ropes, and I'm the best in my gym class."

I believed that.

"First," she said. "I need to do this."

She unbuckled one strap from the bib of her overalls. Then the other strap.

"What are you doing?"

"I can't climb up there with these overalls on."

I couldn't believe it. Rachel was going to take off her clothes in front of me. Would she be naked underneath? Was this really happening?

She pulled down the front bib. I could see she wore a T-shirt underneath. Then she pulled the overalls all the way down. She wore a pair of panties underneath. Her legs were bare. She stood in front of me. If I thought she was beautiful before, she was even more beautiful now.

She grabbed the rope with one hand and then the other. She shimmied up as if she had been doing it all her life. Within seconds, she was at the top, where I hooked the rope.

She yelled down to me.

"I'm about five feet from the exit. I can't make it the rest of the way."

"I think the root will hold both of us. Maybe I can come up and give you a leg up out of here. I think that's about the only way."

As I started up, she shouted, "Come on, slow poke!"

"I'm going as fast as I can."

I finally made it up there. Where it took her seconds, it took me many minutes. I stood on the root and held her tight. I could have held her longer, but I said, "Give me your leg. I'll boost you up."

I had never been in such close contact with a girl before. I was thinking maybe it'd be a good thing if we didn't get out right away. When I gave her a boost, she was out in seconds.

She laid down face first with her head and hands in the hole and said, "Give me your hand."

I grabbed on, and she pulled me up.

"What am I going to tell my folks?" she said. "I'm late for the rest of my chores. I'd better go face the music."

"My music will probably be prettier than yours because I've done all my chores. You still have to do yours."

"I still have to slop out the gutters behind the cows. You know what a hell of a mess they make."

"There's just one thing," I said.

"What's that?" she asked.

"Actually, two things. Shep is still down in the cave. We have to get her out."

"Oh yeah, that's right."

"And the other thing is, your overalls are down there. What would your parents think if you came home almost naked?"

"Oh, they've seen me like this before."

"But with me?"

"How would they know?"

We went down to the front of the gully to dig out the entrance. There stood my uncle, her father, her brother, and Shep. How did Shep get out? The opening was still blocked.

"Did Shep fetch you?" Rachel asked.

"No, she was sitting here when we got here. Your brother said you were fooling around with some boy in this cave."

"We weren't fooling around in the cave. We got trapped in there. I think Fred trapped us in there," Rachel said.

"And look at you. You're almost naked."

"I had to take my overalls off to get out of the cave. We need to go in and get them."

Her dad said, "They can stay in there forever. As far as I'm concerned, this cave can stay blocked up."

He grabbed Rachel's arm and marched her out of the gully.

My uncle said, "I don't think I'm going to like that boy very much. To be honest with you, I'm not so sure about his sister either."

"She's okay. Besides, she's older than me. Why would she be interested in me anyway?"

"You'd be surprised."

CHAPTER 9

THE PHONE CALL

That night, I went over to see Rachel. This time she was wearing a sundress. At least, I think that's what people call them. She was more beautiful every time I saw her.

She said, "What are you doing here? My dad isn't too happy with you."

"I think we need to call the sheriff about the skull. Uncle John doesn't have a phone. Maybe we could use yours."

"Will the sheriff be there this late?"

"Someone should be."

I'd never used a telephone because our family didn't have one either. She pointed me to a black object on the hall table.

"What do I do now?"

"You pick it up and dial," she said.

"How do I do that?"

"You look at the numbers in the little dial and twirl. Like this."

She demonstrated by putting her finger in the eight and turning the dial.

"Maybe you'd better do it," I said.

"You're old enough, and it's about time you learned how to do this," she said as she laughed. I could tell she was having fun at my expense. "Here's the number for the sheriff's office."

"But this doesn't have all numbers. It starts with two letters."

"There are letters inside the dial that correspond to numbers. Use that number."

"That's just silly. Why don't they use numbers in the first place? It would be so much easier."

"Just dial the number."

I did as she instructed. Nothing happened.

"You have to pick up the handset and wait for the dial tone."

"I knew that," I said. "I was just kidding."

Not really, but I wasn't going to let her know that.

I dialed the number, and a woman answered.

"Hello, Sheriff."

"No, this is Mrs. Krocak."

"Sorry," I said and hung up the phone.

"Wrong number, huh? Try again."

I dialed again. A different woman answered.

"Hello. This is the sheriff's office."

"I found a skull," I said.

"Then you probably want to speak to Sheriff Hedrick."

"Yes, please."

"Hold on."

I waited a while until a man got onto the phone.

"Sheriff Hedrick speaking."

"Hello, Sheriff. I found a skull in the field while picking rocks with my grandfather. My grandpa thinks it was an animal skull, but it looked like a human skull like I saw in school."

"You bring it to me, and we'll examine it to see if it is a human skull."

"That's just it. I lost it."

I looked over at Rachel, who had a hand over her mouth to keep from laughing. I had a difficult time keeping from laughing myself.

"You lost it?"

"Well, I didn't lose it. My grandfather threw it in the weeds."

Rachel burst out laughing. That's when I started laughing too.

"Listen, son. We don't have time for these prank calls," he said and hung up.

"You've never used the phone before, have you?" Rachel said.

"You were no help with your laughing."

"You sounded nervous."

"I guess I was. I would have been nervous talking to the sheriff in person anyway," I said.

"I suppose you would. What now?"

"It looks like we have to find that skull before we talk to him again. I've got to get back in the cave."

"How? The entrance is blocked."

"Shep found another way out. I'm going to find it."

She walked me out to the front porch. Probably to protect me if her father showed up.

"Let me know when. I'll go with you. Goodnight."

She twirled to walk into the house. The back of her skirt lifted up, exposing her thigh just an inch. That was more exciting to me than seeing her bare legs when we got out of the cave. I figured this was going to be a very interesting summer.

CHAPTER 10

ASPARAGUS

Rachel and I met the following day.

I pulled something from the bib of my overalls.

"I just remembered something."

"What's that?" Rachel asked.

"I found a letter while walking through the ditch looking for the skull. It was addressed to our neighbor down the road, Mrs. Krauss. I was going to put it in her mailbox, but I forgot. Something distracted me."

"You mean me?"

"Could be, anyway, I forgot."

"Let me see it," she said.

"Did you see where it's from?"

I said, "No, I didn't."

"It looks like it's sent from Elmer Krauss. We'd better get this letter to her."

We walked along the road. Shep followed us, interested in what we were doing. She chased a rabbit in the ditch.

"Look," I said, "There's some wild asparagus."

"It grows wild?"

"Yeah. It's the best asparagus. People hunt all around for it. It tastes better than anything you get in any store."

"Maybe because it's free," she joked.

"On the way back, let's pick some for Uncle John and some for your family."

"I hate asparagus. But I'll have to try this."

We came to Mrs. Krauss's mailbox a half mile down the road. We turned into her short driveway. She was sitting on her porch, fanning herself from the heat of the hot summer day. She was about sixty years old, wore thick glasses, and had her hair up in a kerchief. She was wearing a shawl, probably to protect her from a wind that wasn't there.

"Why does she wear a shawl like that?" Rachel asked.

"It might be a habit from when she grew up. Her parents probably told her to wear a shawl whenever she went outside."

Mrs. Krauss used a white handkerchief to wipe her brow. She looked up when she saw us walking up her driveway.

"What are you two kids doing here? Shouldn't you be out playing or working?"

"We found this letter in the ditch. It's addressed to you."

"Who's it from, I wonder?" she said.

"It looks like it's from Elmer Krauss."

"That's my son. He's in the service in Vietnam. I've been expecting his letter. Bring it up to me, would you please?"

We both walked up onto the steps. Mrs. Krauss took the envelope and looked at it.

"Oh, dear. I haven't got my glasses. Would you mind opening it and reading it to me?"

"I don't know. I don't feel right reading your private mail," I said.

Rachel grabbed the letter and said, "I'll read it."

She carefully opened the letter. She didn't rip it apart as I did to letters addressed to me when I was anxious to see what was inside.

It says, "Dear Mom, Just a letter to let you know that I'm okay. Things are pretty hectic here. There's a lot of fighting going on. I haven't been involved in any yet, but I expect to be soon. The hikes through the jungle are no walks in the woods, I tell you that. We are careful as we can be. I'm praying nothing will happen to me. Love, Elmer."

Mrs. Krauss said, "And I'm praying nothing will happen to him. I told him he should tell me like it is. After all, I know things are dangerous over there. I read the newspapers about how many of our boys are killed and wounded."

I hadn't been paying attention to what was happening in Vietnam. I should have since my brother was over there too.

"Maybe he's in the same company as my brother," I said.

"It could be. Those two went in at the same time."

"Why are we over there anyway?" Rachel asked.

"To protect our country from the Communists. We don't want them over here."

"Who says they'll even come over here?" Rachel asked.

"Our leaders know much more about it than we do. We must trust in them. I hear it won't be more than a few months, and they'll be back home where they belong."

"They should never have left."

"Oh, look," Mrs. Krauss said. "This letter was dated weeks ago. It's been in that ditch a long time."

I said, "I only found it in the ditch the other day."

"I haven't been getting a lot of my mail. Even some bills that I needed to pay."

"My mom says we're missing some mail too."

"I don't know about Uncle John. He never tells me anything. I'll ask him."

"It could be somebody going through our mailboxes looking for money."

"Or some kids out on a joy ride and playing pranks," I said.

"Thank you for bringing the letter to me. I've been so worried that I haven't heard from him for a long time. I know he'll be home soon."

"Do you have a grocery bag? We found some wild asparagus. Maybe you'd like some?"

"I'll get you some bags, but I can't stand the stuff."

Then, it came to me.

"Did you ever know anyone by the name Marek Kniha?"

"No, why do you ask?"

"We want to find out about someone with that name who lived in a cave around here."

"Lived in a cave! No. Why would anyone do that?"

"That's a good question," I said.

"There were a lot of Mareks around here. My father-in-law's first name was Marek, but he was a Patek. You should ask your uncle."

We headed back after filling the two bags. When we got to Uncle John's place, Rachel continued up the hill to her home. I found Uncle John sitting on his rocking chair. He was calculating board feet of lumber in his head from memory. I don't know how he did that. I guess from years of practice from his sawmill.

"I got you some wild asparagus from the ditch."

"I didn't expect those to be up yet. As a reward, you can help me with the baling tomorrow."

I wondered what my reward would have been if I hadn't brought him anything.

The next day as we walked out to the machine shed, I asked, "What do you know about this war in Vietnam?"

"Nothing. And I don't want to know."

"Why not?"

"Because I was in World War I. Your dad was in World War II, and now your brother is fighting in a war, and that's enough from us. I hope you don't have to go into a war. It's not any fun."

"Then why do we do it? Why are there wars?"

"Because people who think they are smarter than we are figure that war is the best way to solve some problems in the world. The young people in each country fight to see who is right."

I said, "I think if they want to find out who was right, they should have the oldest people fight. The ones who are making decisions."

"We voted them in. We have to do as they say."

"The people who voted for them should have to do the fighting."

"In a perfect world, that's the way it would be. As it has been from the beginning of time, it's the young people dying for the mistakes of others."

"You think that war is a mistake?"

"I think anything that causes needless death is a mistake. Why do you ask?"

"We were at Mrs. Krauss's today. She got a letter from her son in Vietnam. I found it when we were looking for the skull."

"Did you find any of my letters there?"

"No, we didn't."

"I'm missing some mail too. Perhaps, when you get a chance, you can look through the ditch and see if you can find anything addressed to me."

"What are you missing?" I asked.

"I'm missing my Social Security check."

"Why would they take other people's checks?"

"To cash them for the money."

"How could someone cash a check that is made out to someone else?"

"When people want something bad enough, they figure out a way."

"Did you know anyone by the name Marek Kniha?"

"Can't say as I did. Are you sure you got that right? Kniha is the Czech word for book."

This was great. Kniha wasn't his last name. This Marek could be anybody.

"Do you know of any Marek who lived in a cave?"

"Now you got me there. I've never heard of such a thing. You know who you might ask is your grandfather. He's been around a lot longer than me."

After baling, I found my grandfather feeding chickens.

"What you up to, Jimmie?"

"I'm still trying to find out about that skull."

"What skull?"

"The one we found when we were picking rocks."

"All we found was rocks, Jimmie."

"Okay," I said, deciding to change course. My grandfather would never admit he was wrong. "Do you remember anybody named Marek who used to live in a cave?"

"I don't know anyone named Marek who lived in a cave."

"I had to ask," I said.

"Since you ask, I did hear of someone else living in a cave. I heard about it from Marek Patek. Mrs. Krauss's father-in-law. He told me once some Bohunk was living in a cave by the gully."

"He did. Who?"

"He didn't say. Marek was drunk when he told me, and I never believed a word of it."

CHAPTER 11

THE ICEHOUSE

That afternoon, I walked out of the chicken coop carrying a bucket of eggs. I looked up and saw Rachel. She had her hands on her hips. She wore a floral shirt, shorts, and tennis shoes.

She looked at me and asked, "When are we going to look for the skull?"

"I have to do some more chores first."

"The hell with your chores. I want to find that opening and get into that cave. I brought a flashlight along so we can explore."

I set the basket of eggs down, which probably wasn't the smartest thing to do. Rachel distracted me so much I wasn't paying attention. I had gotten about a few steps away when a raccoon knocked over the eggs and was eating them. Uncle John wasn't going to be happy about this. Right then, I didn't care. My mind was on Rachel. I guess the cave opening was too.

Rachel said, "Wait a second. I wasn't going to tell you but I found a note in the ditch. It warned us to stop looking."

"Where is it?"

"I threw it away because I don't want to stop."

"Then neither do I."

We marched out towards the gully. We walked through the woods, following a path the cows had worn down over years and years of heading out to pasture.

"Is your brother going to be bothering us today?"

"No, I made sure of that."

"How did you do that?"

"My folks were going to town. I talked them into taking him along. He likes to go to town. He gets to go to the store and buys a bottle of pop. Then he gets comic books and reads them while my parents do all their other shopping. So I don't think we'll see him for the rest of the day."

"That's good because he caused too much trouble yesterday. I wonder what he would have done to us today."

"Now you know what I go through each day," she said.

"I'm glad I don't have a brother like that. He would just as soon ignore me as anything else."

"You're lucky."

The trees were starting to bloom. The smell of blossoms was in the air, mingled with the odor of manure. Along the path to the gully, I saw the opening that we crawled out of yesterday.

She said, "I suppose if we can't find the opening that Shep got out of, you could just lower me down in there."

"I want to explore that cave a little more too. I hope we find the other opening. I mean, if Shep could find it, we should too."

"Hey, where is Shep?"

I yelled for Shep. She could help us find the opening, but there was no Shep. "Where is that dog? Usually, she knows that I need her somehow, and she's around."

"It must be good to have a dog like that."

We got to the front of the cave. It was still blocked up. That wasn't surprising. It wasn't magically going to unblock itself.

"Do you think it's a good idea to pursue this skull thing anymore?" she asked.

"I don't think so. Nothing good will come from it."

"You're right."

"I'm going to anyway," I said.

"Yeah. Me too."

"I don't feel like unblocking the entrance here. We need to find the way that Shep used."

We searched one side of the gully with no luck. I yelled for Shep again. Still no Shep. Where was that dog? Then I heard a bark. It was from inside the cave! Shep was in the cave. What was she doing in there?

She must know where the opening is because she got in again somehow. Perhaps if we yelled for her and looked, we could see where she exits the cave. I shouted for Shep again. There was no answer.

"I think she might be coming out. Keep your eyes peeled and see where she's coming from."

We waited and looked and looked. There still was no sign of Shep.

"Maybe she isn't coming out."

"I don't know what to think. Maybe Shep's in there waiting for us to come inside."

I heard something behind me. I turned to look. There was Shep, sitting at our feet behind us and panting.

"I didn't see where she came out. It can't be too far away."

"I don't know. Shep runs pretty fast."

We searched the other side of the gully. Shep just followed us. Shep knew where the opening was, but she wasn't going to tell us. We searched around the other side and came upon an opening. We looked inside, but it was just a little hole a fox or some animal had dug out for protection from the snow in the winter or rain in the summer.

"This isn't it. I had hoped it might be."

She said, "Yeah, let's keep looking."

We wandered around a little more, and we came to a building that consisted of old logs. All the doors and windows were out. The roof and sides were still okay.

"I think I know what this was," I said. "My uncle told me they used to bring ice blocks from Plum Creek and store it here."

"An icehouse."

"Yeah. Let's not go inside. It doesn't look any too safe."

She went in anyway, and I followed. Inside, it was very dark.

"Turn on your flashlight," I said.

"What's that in the corner?"

"It looks like it's a hole of some sort."

"Do you think it might lead into the cave?"

"Yeah, I think so."

We crawled into the opening. It wasn't big enough for us to stand. However, it was easy enough for Shep to walk through. After about ten to fifteen feet, it opened up to a wide tunnel. Just then we were left in the dark.

"Great. I think the battery died," she said.

"Now what?"

"We need to get another flashlight."

"You're right. Mine's back in the house," I said.

"And we don't even have the candles."

"We should go back."

She must have been eager to explore because she continued ahead in the dark. So I did too. We walked in the darkness for what seemed like an hour. Maybe it was only about five or ten minutes. Then, we came to a wall.

"I thought that this was it. It's a dead end, and Shep couldn't have come through here. Maybe we missed something in the dark."

We turned around and tried to walk back from where we had come. After about a minute, another wall blocked our way. That didn't work. We turned again and walked at a right angle. We arrived at another dead end. We were lost.

CHAPTER 12

THE BOHUNK'S ROOM

If we weren't trapped yesterday, we were trapped now.

I said, "Somehow, we missed the opening to the main part of the cave."

"What do we do now?"

"Where's Shep?"

I didn't hear Shep, so I yelled out for her, but there was no sign of her.

"She's probably waiting for us outside or in the part of the cave we should have gone."

"What do we do now?"

"I guess we wander around until we get to where we want to be."

We took another right turn and walked at an angle. We came to another dead end.

I said, "You know, I don't know if we came to the first dead end or if it's a new one."

A few steps ahead, my foot banged into something, and I stubbed my toe hard.

"What happened?" she asked.

"I ran into something. I'm reaching down, and I'm touching something flat. I think it's a table. And here is a chair. Rachel, I think we're in that room where I found the journal."

She said, "Yeah, I think you're right because I'm sitting on the bed. Let's call this the Bohunk's room."

"It seems we're better off than we were a few minutes ago. We aren't lost. We know where we are. Now we have to return to where we left the candles. Below the hole where we crawled out yesterday."

"You know, we wandered around so much we'll never find how we got here from the opening in the icehouse," she said.

"Yeah, but at least we know there's an opening now. That's something,"

"Yeah, and we know we can get out of here if necessary. Like we did yesterday."

"There is that."

"Of course, I'm not sure I want to try that again," she said.

I would have been willing to do that once more.

"Maybe if we had some candles, we could find our way to the icehouse opening."

"You said you could feel your way back to that by touching the walls. Here's your chance."

I had to prove to her that I could do it.

I said, "Follow me."

"I can't see you."

"Here's my hand."

I reached back for her hand. She groped and touched my back and ended up touching my butt.

"Oops, sorry."

"That's okay," I said. And it was.

She reached for my hand and held onto it. I had to get my bearings straight. I knew the direction to take from the table. I started walking. We got about ten steps and she yelled.

"What happened?" I asked.

"You walked me into a wall."

"Sorry about that."

We walked along, taking lefts and rights. Gradually we began to see a little light. We continued until we saw an opening up ahead. There we saw the candles and matches. Just below the opening, I saw her overalls.

"Let's explore more of the cave," I said.

This time we had the lit candle to better see where we were going. Rachel no longer had to have her hand on my butt. I mean, she no longer had to hold my hand.

In the Bohunk's room, we searched for the journal and the skull. It was difficult to see much of anything in the dim light of the candles.

"We need to return later with our flashlights," I said.

We took a few wrong turns. It seemed like we found branches of the cave we had never seen before. Finally, we saw a faint light up ahead. I figured the light must be from the entrance we used in the icehouse. I had feared that it also might be sealed up.

I said, "I don't get it. Why is someone so worried about us finding the skull when I don't even have it?"

"Whoever it is doesn't know that."

"If I don't have it, who does? Your brother?"

"If it were my brother, you'd certainly know about it."

"Maybe some wild animal carried it off."

"Why would it carry off a skull?"

"You know, when we get out, we should search that part of the field again to see what else we might find."

CHAPTER 13

IT COULD BE ANYWHERE

When we left the cave, we found Shep waiting outside. We headed toward the field where I found the skull. I was pretty sure I remembered exactly where it was. My footprints would be there if nothing else. When we got out there, my uncle had decided that this was the day he would disk the field. All the evidence was gone.

"Figures, doesn't it?" I said.

"Yeah, it figures. Do you have any idea where it might be?"

"It could be anywhere."

"Brilliant," she said. "Everything could be anywhere."

I went to the spot where I thought it might be. I remembered a huge rock off to one side and angled off toward the area in the ditch where I had been searching before. We searched around there for a little while and found nothing. My uncle probably destroyed it with the disk. That's if anything had been there.

"Let's go look out in the ditch again," I said.

We went out to the ditch, where I had searched a couple of times before. We went back and forth and found empty cans and bottles.

"Did you look over there?" Rachel asked.

"No. That's nowhere near where my uncle tossed the skull."

"Why does that matter?"

"I guess it doesn't."

After a few minutes, Rachel picked up an old purse. It was weathered as if it had been in the weeds for months.

"This looks like it was thrown in the ditch a long time ago," she said.

"I wonder if there's anything inside."

"There's only one way to find out." She opened the purse. "There's nothing in here. No wallet. No Identification of any kind. Wait! Here's a receipt. I can read the writing. It's from Tikalsky's store in New Prague. It's dated about a year ago."

"I wonder what she bought," I asked.

"On the bottom of the receipt, it says she bought a purse. Probably this purse."

"Do you think if we went there, we could find out who lost the purse?"

"That's the plan," she said.

"What good would it do us?"

"Maybe they might know who bought the purse."

"That's a stretch," I said.

"Yeah, but it's the only stretch we have."

"I guess so. Let's call it a day."

"No," she said. "Let's look a little more."

We kicked through the area where we had found the purse. There was a shoe. It also seemed weathered like it had spent the winter hiding out there.

"Why do I see shoes along the side of the road all the time?" I asked.

"Is it by people with only one foot? Why else throw a perfectly good shoe out the car window? This is a perfectly good shoe."

I said, "It's not like it's worn out or anything. My mom would have worn that for another year or two."

"She would never wear this. It looks too uncomfortable."

"If the shoe fits, wear it, my dad would say."

"You have a point there," she said.

"Yeah. If I part my hair right."

"Now that we found this much, we should keep looking."

She went in one direction. I went in the other. I came upon old sunglasses.

"This is weird," I said. "A purse. A shoe. Sunglasses. I don't know what it means, but it's like someone was cleaning out a car."

"Yes. It's like someone was trying to get rid of evidence. We found this much. Let's keep looking."

We wandered around and came upon the most exciting item of the day. It was a wallet that looked like it came with the purse.

"Now we're getting somewhere. Let's look inside."

Inside we found three dollars, but nothing else. We had about given up when Rachel said, "There's a hidden compartment!"

"What's inside?"

"No driver's license. Just a picture of a pretty girl with long, curly blonde hair. The name Jezebel is written on the back."

"Jezebel. Now there's a hell of a name for you," I said.

"Jezebel might be the person who lost the purse and the wallet. Could that be the same person who belongs to the skull?"

"There's one way to find out. We could call the sheriff to see if this person has been missing," I said.

"We could do that. Or we could go to Tikalsky's with this picture and this receipt and see if they know the person that belongs to it. That would be more fun."

"How are we going to get to Tikalsky's?"

"It's a long way to town."

"I know! My uncle is going to town to grind feed later this morning. That's what he said. We could ride into town with him," I said.

"Maybe your uncle knows who this is."

"We'll try that first."

Later we asked my uncle about Jezebel, and my uncle had no idea who she was. He did talk us into calling the sheriff to ask if anyone named Jezebel had gone missing. We got on the line with a very uncooperative woman when we reached the sheriff's department. She treated us as though we were pulling a prank. I would have asked more questions if I had been her. She said nobody was missing by that name, and if there was, what was it to us?

I said to Rachel, "It could have been someone just passing through town."

"Most likely. The woman was right, though. What's it to us?"

CHAPTER 14

YOU'D BE SURPRISED

Later that morning, we rode in the truck heading to New Prague. My uncle pulled up next to the feed mill, and we jumped out. We ran to Tikalsky's. I don't know why we were running. I guess we were just excited and anxious to find out about Jezebel. After we entered the door, I asked a clerk about the receipt.

She said, "Let me look at that. Oh, my goodness, that's from a year ago. What would we know about a receipt from a year ago?"

"It looks like she might have bought this purse and wallet here."

"Oh, yes, we carry those purses. If you want the money back, I don't think we can give it to you. It's a completely worn-out purse."

"No, we don't want the money back. We're wondering if you know who might have bought it?"

"I didn't sell it. These are all handwritten receipts. You see? And my signature isn't on the bottom. It's Clara's handwriting and her signature. She might know."

"Is she here?"

"She comes in at four and it's noon now."

"We'll be back then. Thanks."

I said to Rachel, "We could wait around town, but my uncle's going to want to head back. He isn't going to wait around for us to find this Jezebel."

"We can find another ride back somehow," she said.

"I'll tell my uncle we'll visit my folks in town until four o'clock. You'll like them."

"You don't have a bratty brother?"

"No, my bratty brother is in the service."

We walked across town to my parent's place. When we got there, we walked right in. My mom, in her forties and heavy set, was sitting in the living room. She was watching a soap opera called *All My Children,* a show she followed religiously.

"Hi, Jimmie. Did you bring Shep along?" she asked, looking at the floor. She had a habit of not looking at anyone when she talked,

"No, I brought Rachel."

"Rachel. Who's Rachel?"

"Just some girl."

"Oh, thanks a lot," Rachel said.

"I mean, she's a girl whose family just moved in next to Uncle John's place."

"Well, I'm glad to meet you, just some girl. Sit down. You want something to eat?"

The house was in its usual state of disarray. Clothes were lying about. Dirty dishes were all over the coffee table in the living room. My mom went into the kitchen. Rachel followed her with the dishes.

"Let me help you with these," Rachel said. She went to the sink, poured some tap water, and added soap. "I'll wash these while you make the sandwich."

"Oh, you don't have to do that."

"My mom said I should always help out. There's no free lunch."

"This isn't lunch. It's dinner," my mom said.

"Dinner is at six o'clock."

"No, six o'clock is supper."

"Oh yeah, that's right. You're missing your show."

"That's okay. It's the same thing every day."

"Too bad you can't stop the show and watch it later."

"That'll never happen."

By the time Rachel finished the dishes, my mom had put the sandwiches and glasses of milk on the table. After Rachel sat down, she took a sip of the milk. A funny look came to her face. I didn't know what was happening, but then I took a drink of milk. It was sour. I couldn't have Rachel drink this and get sick. That would be something, wouldn't it?

There was only one thing to do. I got up quickly and jarred the table. Both glasses tipped over, emptying the glasses.

"That was the end of the milk," my mom said.

I figured it was the end of the milk days ago.

"The coffee is still warm. You could drink that. You can't eat without drinking something."

As we ate, Rachel put down her sandwich and looked at my mom.

"Do you know of anybody by the name of Jezebel?"

"From the Bible?"

"No, not from the Bible. From around here."

"I know a Jesse and a Belle. Unless the two became one person and became Jezebel, I don't think I can help you."

"No one seems to know who she is, Mom."

"Why are you looking for her?"

"I think she lost her purse, and we're trying to get it back to her."

"That's nice of you. I hope you find her. How are you going to get it back to her?"

"At Tikalsky's store, they said they might know who bought this purse a while ago. Maybe they can help us," Rachel said.

"Yeah, that's a good idea. I hope it works. It sounds like something you see on television."

"On television, they find the person, but I don't think we'll have much luck," I said.

"You're a lucky kid, Jimmie." She looked over at Rachel. "A real lucky kid."

Rachel left to go to the bathroom. My mom looked at me. "She's a keeper."

"A keeper? I don't even have her."

"You'd be surprised."

CHAPTER 15

WHAT'S IN STORE

We went to Tikalsky's to see if we could find out more about Jezebel. When we entered the store, we saw the clerk we had seen earlier. It was four o'clock, so Clara should have been back. Had we waited around for nothing? That would have been a waste of time. We decided to look around the store for a little while until that clerk was free from waiting on her customer.

An old woman was buying some cloth.

"I'm making something for my son. It's going to be a shirt for school."

I looked at the cloth. It was the weirdest design. It was the ugliest piece of material that I've ever seen. If she made a shirt from that stuff and her son wore it to school, I felt sorry for him.

Finally, she decided on just how much she wanted. She bought the whole roll. She must have had one big son. Maybe it was for two shirts.

When it came time to pay, she said, "Put it on my account."

She picked up her bag with the cloth and left. We rushed up to the clerk.

"Is Clara here?"

"Yes, she is. She's in the back. I told her about you," she said. "Maybe you should talk to her."

She went in the back. A few minutes later, she and a woman who must have been Clara finally came out.

"Can I help you two?" Clara said, with a heavy Czech accent.

"Yeah, we're looking for a girl who might have bought a purse here. This purse."

Clara picked it up and examined it through thick, wire-rimmed glasses. She held it with her thumb and forefinger by a corner as if she might catch some strange disease. She looked at it closely and said, "Yes. These are the purses that we sell here."

"Here. Look at this receipt. It has your name on it."

She said, "It sure does. It's from a year ago. How can I help you? You don't want your money back, do you? This purse is way too old. We can't give you the money back for this."

"No, it's not that. Like we told the other woman, we were wondering if you knew who you sold this purse to."

She looked at me and said, "You know, son. If I had a nickel for every purse I've sold, I'd be a rich woman."

The other clerk said, "Clara, you get more than a nickel for every purse you sell."

"Oh yeah, that's right. But I'm not rich. I might not remember her. I mean, how could I? It's been a year or so."

"Here. We've got her picture. We found it in the wallet. It has the name Jezebel on the back."

"Jezebel. You know. That sounds familiar. Let me think. She was only eighteen years old. Maybe even just a high school girl. You see, the thing is. We usually only get local people in the store, and she wasn't local. That's why I can sort of remember the conversation."

"You can?" Rachel asked.

Clara said, "When I asked the girl if she was new in town, she said she wasn't from around here. She told me her name was Jezebel but wouldn't tell me her last name."

Rachel asked, "Did she say where she was going?"

"She told me she was headed to Shakopee. She had an uncle who had a bar there called the Spot Bar. That's all I know about Jezebel."

Rachel said, "That's more than we even expected."

"Yes," I said. "You've helped us out a lot."

"I'm glad I could help. Is there anything else I can do for you?"

I felt a little guilty about taking her time and not buying anything.

"How about a bag of that licorice there."

"That I can do for you. How much do you want?"

"Fifty cents worth."

As she dished out the huge bag of licorice, she asked, "Anything else?"

"And that Gravy Train for my dog Shep."

I paid for the dog food and licorice. Before we left, I asked, "Is that woman serious about making a boy's shirt out of that material she bought?"

Clara said, "I think so."

"It looks more like material for a girl."

"You know, I was thinking the same thing, but I wasn't going to tell her that."

Rachel said, "It's awful. Plus an awful lot of it too."

"I was thinking that too," she said. "Sometimes they're embarrassed to say it's for themselves. They don't like to buy stuff for themselves, so they say it's for their kid or their husband or something."

Rachel said, "You'd think a woman should be able to buy anything she wants for herself without feeling guilty."

"Oh, most of these Czech wives buy what they want. You know how some husbands are. They figure they do all the work and make all the money, and the women don't do anything for it."

Rachel said, "I think it should be the other way around. I think the husband is the one who should be going without."

"That's why I haven't married. I guess that's why I have this store. My money is my money, and I don't have to answer to any man. For anything."

Rachel said, "You know what my mom says?"

"What does she say?"

"A good woman is as good as any man. A bad woman is the equal of two men."

"That's the strangest thing I ever heard. It makes no sense."

"That's the way my mom is. She's sort of funny that way."

"I'd like to meet her. I don't recognize you. Are you new in town?"

"Actually, yes, I just moved in next to Jimmie's uncle's place."

"Oh. The Svieg's old farm."

"I don't know if that's it, but that's where we are."

"I think you're going to like it there. They were good people. Too bad they had to move into town. They were getting sort of old to run that farm."

"My folks are young. They should be able to handle it."

"I'm sure they will. Enjoy your licorice."

"We will."

When we left, Rachel said, "Now we know something more than we did before. We know she has an uncle in Shakopee at the Spot Bar. That's if Jezebel was telling the truth."

"Why wouldn't she?"

"She might not want anyone to know where she's going. She could be trying to throw people off her track."

"Why would she be doing that?" I asked.

"Jezebel is a runaway."

"I can't imagine anyone doing that."

"She probably didn't like it at home and left for some reason. I'm glad I don't have to do that. I sort of like it at my house, and I have good parents."

I said, "I guess we're lucky that way."

"We sure are."

"So, what next?"

"I think we need to make a trip to Shakopee to the Spot Bar," Rachel said.

"How are we going to get away to do something like that? And how are we going to get there?"

"We're going to hitchhike."

"My mom says hitchhiking is dangerous."

"It's dangerous, but we'll be okay because there are two of us. If there were just one of us, I'd be afraid."

I said, "Yes. I'll protect you."

"I thought I would have to protect you, little kid."

"Little kid!"

"Just kidding. I know you're younger than me, but you look much older."

I was happy to hear that she thought that. If she thought I looked younger than her little brother, it would be difficult being with her.

"When are we going to do this?" I asked.

"How about tomorrow?"

"Tomorrow. I think I can do that. I'll come up with some excuse for Uncle John. You come up with some excuse for your parents. We'll head out as early in the morning as we can."

"It's a good idea. I'll meet you at the end of your uncle's driveway at eight in the morning."

Rachel asked, "How do we get home now?"

"My dad should just be getting off work. He can give us a ride. Besides he'll want to meet you anyway."

"I hope it goes better than when you met *my* dad."

CHAPTER 16

WHICH WAY TO LYDIA

Rachel was already waiting for me the following day when I got there.

"We're going to have to walk a little way. We won't get a ride from here," I said.

Just then, a car pulled up next to us.

"Need a ride?"

It was Joe Svoboda, a neighbor who lived down the road. I guess we didn't have to wait too long after all.

"Where are you headed?" he asked.

"We're going to Shakopee."

"I can take you as far as Lydia. That's where I'm going. After that, you're on your own."

"No, we're not. There's the two of us."

"I mean, you'll have to find your own way after that. It's halfway."

"My Uncle John says halfway is better than no way."

When we both got in the back seat, Svoboda said, "Hell, I ain't no chauffeur. You two get up in front here with me."

I got up in the roomy front seat and sat next to him. Rachel sat next to the passenger door.

"It's a nice car."

"Yep. Got it brand new last month. I figure I'll get a lot of miles out of this. Maybe even ten thousand."

"That's a lot of miles to get out of a car. My uncle's lucky to get half that many on his cars."

"His problem is he buys used cars. I buy brand new ones."

"My uncle says he can't afford a new car."

"He can't afford *not* to have a new car. Old ones just break down and get flat tires."

"Yeah. Sakra Menske."

"Hey, watch your language!"

I told him the story about how my uncle called a flat tire a Sakra Menske."

He said, "In my family, it's Jezis Maria."

"That's Jesus Mary. Do you know what Sakra Menske means?" I asked.

"I do, but if I tell you, I'll go to hell."

"Then you better not tell me."

We were about to drive through Saint Patrick. On the right was the Saint Patrick ballpark. In the outfield, left field wasn't flat. It sloped uphill toward the foul line. Many outfielders fell on their faces trying to run up toward the foul line to catch a ball. Easy outs were turned into doubles or triples.

Behind home plate, it went uphill as well. On a passed ball or wild pitch, the catcher would just turn around and wait for the ball to come back down the hill toward him. A lot of the parks in these small towns were built like that. Saint Benedict had a short right-field fence because of a creek that bordered the park. The right-handed hitters would turn around and bat left-handed so they could loft easy fly balls over that fence for a home run.

I said, "I like these old parks."

"I started up the DRS League a few years ago. Made up of teams from towns in Dakota, Rice, and Scott Counties. The teams have good players just from their little towns. Saint Patrick has a team of Nashes, Vaughns, Friedges, and DeGrosses. It's a fun, fun league. New Market will be the best team. They've got all the Schmitz boys. Damn good players. Oh, sorry. I didn't mean to swear."

"That's okay, I've heard worse," Rachel said.

"I shouldn't be talking like that in front of a young girl."

"Like I said. I've heard worse."

Approaching the corner to Fish Lake, I saw the little store where they sold bait and pop and candy. My dad would always stop there to buy bait on our way to Fish Lake. We haven't done that in a while. We'd take along an eight-gallon milk can filled with water. We'd fish offshore for sunnies and bullheads and toss them into the milk can. When we were done fishing, my dad would cut up a few of those, fry them up, and we'd eat along the shore. My mom would bring some potato salad, pop, and beer. When we got home, my grandfather would clean the bullheads. I tried that once, but I stabbed my hand on those stickers on the side. I never cleaned bullheads again.

I wouldn't be surprised if that little corner store didn't have a baseball team eventually.

As we neared Lydia, I asked, "Is Lydia going to have a team?"

"No, it isn't big enough."

To me, it looked bigger than Saint Patrick.

He said, "This is where I stop. I'll let you off here. You know how to get to Shakopee?"

"Sure do. My folks go there often enough to visit my grandma."

"Just stop in and see her. She probably isn't going to be around long. You know how that goes."

I didn't, but I said, "Yeah, I know how that goes."

"Just stay out of the bars, and you'll be okay."

"We're too young for that," I said.

"I was never too young for that," Svoboda said.

CHAPTER 17

THE SPOT BAR

Svoboda let us off, and we stood at the side of Highway 13. For the longest time, no cars stopped. They just zoomed past us. Then one stopped right next to us. It was one that I wished hadn't stopped. It was a Scott County Deputy Sheriff's car.

"What do you think you're doing?" he asked.

"Uh, we're going to Shakopee."

"No, you aren't. You can't be hitchhiking along this road or anywhere else."

I said, "We made it to Lydia. We don't have that many more miles before we get to Shakopee. I suppose we could walk."

He thought for a second.

"I can't have you hitchhiking along here. Hop in the car. If anyone asks, I didn't give you a ride to Shakopee. That's where I'm headed. That's where our office is."

We got into the deputy's car. Not to be arrested. At least, I didn't think we were. We were headed in the right direction, I think.

"How are you going to get back?"

I said, "My grandma lives there. My uncle too. I can get a ride back with him."

It wasn't true. It was as good an excuse as any. Because if I said we didn't have a ride, who knows where we'd end up? Maybe spend the night in jail, and our folks would have to come and get us.

"Where are you from?"

"I live in New Prague," I said.

"New Prague! One of my good friends is the policeman there."

"Who is that?"

He said, "Frank Ziska."

I said, "I know him, because he's always arresting my brother."

"Why? What is your brother doing wrong?"

"He can't seem to keep a muffler on his car. He gets all these tickets for not having a muffler. He can put a new muffler on one day, and it'd be off by the side of the road the next day. Your friend, Frank Ziska, here's the thing about him. One time, he stopped my brother for drunken driving. That's one thing you don't want to do."

He said, "Young kids drinking and driving. I'd rather have you hitchhike than that."

"Don't worry. I don't even have a license yet, and I don't drink."

"That's good. You're a smart one."

We were coming down the hill into Shakopee. My mom always called it smoky Shakopee. It did look like there was a big cloud of smoke over the town.

I said, "Do you know where the Spot Bar is?"

"What do you want to know that for?"

"That's where my uncle works as a bartender."

These lies were coming fast and furious.

The deputy said, "I can't drop you off there, but it's a few blocks down the street and take a right another two blocks. You can't miss it."

When somebody tells me I can't miss it, I'm going to miss it.

I said, "We'll find it. Thanks."

After we got out of the car, Rachel said, "Do you have any idea where it is?"

"Not a clue. My dad always says in any town, walk two blocks, and you're bound to find a bar."

He was right. Because down the street, we saw a bar. It wasn't the Spot Bar. It was the Coachman. As we neared the bar, we saw someone coming out. I got an idea.

"Hello, sir. We're looking for the Spot Bar."

"What the hell you going there for? You're not old enough to drink."

"That's what everybody tells us, and we know it, but my dad is there. We're supposed to meet him there."

"It's a hell of a thing. Having your kid meet you at a bar."

"He doesn't do it all the time. Just today."

"Yeah, I've heard that before. Like I've never been to the Spot Bar before. Okay, you go three blocks along here. It'll be on your left. It's got a big, bright, red Schmidt Beer sign on the outside. You can't miss it."

"Okay, thanks. We'll find it."

Three blocks ahead, we saw the Schmidt sign. We got to the entrance, turned, and walked through the door. After the bright sunlight, it was hard to see in the dim light of the bar. We stood there for a while until our eyes became accustomed to the darkness. Then we noticed everyone was looking at us. We were strangers, which was odd enough, but we were also too young to be in there.

"What are you doing in here?" the bartender asked.

"We're looking for the owner."

"He's not here."

"When's he going to be back?"

"He'll be back in an hour. He's taking money to the bank."

It must be nice to have a bar, so you have money to take to the bank.

"Can we wait until he gets back?"

"No. We can't have any minors sitting around here. We'd get in trouble."

We turned and walked out the door.

"I know. We can stop and ask every person that goes in if they're the owner."

"What if he goes in the back way?" she said.

"Okay, you stand out here in front. I'll go out back."

"Sounds like a plan."

I wandered out back. There were garbage cans and an old beat-up car. I saw a man coming to the back door.

"Are you the owner?" I asked.

"I wish."

Next, a woman got out of the car. I didn't ask her, but I thought I'd better. Maybe it was the owner's wife, but it was too late. She'd already gone inside.

Another man came up, wobbling back and forth. I didn't bother asking him either because he looked drunk, and I didn't think the owner would be drunk.

The back door of the bar opened, and I saw Rachel. She was accompanied by a small man with a graying beard and heavy, thick glasses.

Rachel said, "This is the owner."

I said, "You are? Maybe you can help us."

"This is what I was telling the girl. Jezebel was supposed to come here, but she never showed up."

"I was hoping she might be here because then we can return her purse," Rachel said.

He said, "You didn't talk to the sheriff, did you?"

"No," I said, yet another lie,

And I remembered we had just talked to the deputy sheriff. Why didn't we tell him about this?

I said, "We tried calling there, but they thought we were just some kids, and what the hell do we know?"

"You got that right. What are you doing butting your nose into something that isn't your business?"

"What do you mean? We're just trying to find her."

"Did you ever think she doesn't want to be found? She might have run off to Minneapolis or something. If she's found, she'll probably get sent back to a place where she doesn't want to be."

He turned and went into the bar, leaving us standing in the back with the garbage.

"Now what?" Rachel asked.

CHAPTER 18

DON'T LOOK

Rachel and I stood behind the Spot Bar.

"What do we do now?" she asked.

"We hitchhike back home."

"No, I mean, what do we do about Jezebel?"

"It seems nobody wants to find her. Maybe she doesn't want to be found," I said.

"If she's still alive. You're forgetting about the skull."

"She's probably in Minneapolis, happy to be away from her family and whatever she was running away from."

"What about the wallet and purse?"

"Could be she was getting rid of everything that reminded her of her old life," I said.

"Okay, forget it then. Let's get back home."

We walked in silence for a few blocks to the edge of Shakopee. We stopped on the side of the road, waiting for a ride. Storm clouds moved in from the west.

Finally, I said, "Rachel, I'm not giving up. I want to find out what happened to her. I hope we find her alive and well."

"I do too."

"I hope the deputy sheriff doesn't come by before we get a ride," I said.

"Me too."

Cars buzzed past us, not even slowing down. I caught the smell of freshly cut alfalfa.

"I love that smell," Rachel said.

"I do too. But it reminds me of the hard work that comes with it."

"It doesn't look so hard."

"It is. First, you have to cut the alfalfa with a mower that's always breaking down. You have to lift the blade on turns and to avoid rocks. Then after it dries, it's raked into rows for baling. Then you have to hope the baler doesn't break down and the bales aren't coming apart. Then the real fun starts. I stand on the wagon while my uncle tosses the bales up to me. I drag the heavy bales over and stack them. The bottom rows aren't so bad. Try heaving those bales up higher than you are."

"I guess it isn't so much fun."

"The best part is the end of the day when you get to sit under the tree and drink pop and eat bologna sandwiches."

"Bologna sandwiches. That sounds terrible."

"Nothing tastes better than that after a hard day baling. You aren't done yet. You still have the evening milking and chores to do."

"I'd never want to be a farmer."

I was glad to hear that. We didn't have to spend our lives on a farm. Wait. There was no we. Once school started, she would hang around with boys her age. I would sit around with the boys from ninth grade, just waiting to get older. Rachel would always be older than me. This summer was all we would have.

"What do you want to be?" I asked.

"I want to be a doctor."

"A doctor? Only men are doctors."

"Are you living in the dark ages?"

"All I know is the doctors in New Prague are men, so I just figured, that's all."

I hoped we would get a ride before it started to rain. Luckily, a car stopped for us. The driver was an old woman who wore a scowl.

"Get in," she said.

Rachel and I hurried into the back seat and shut the door.

"Normally, I don't pick up hitchhikers. If you two are too stupid to know better what could happen to you, I figure it was smart to pick you up."

I said, "Rachel's smart. She wants to be a doctor."

"That is smart. The world needs more women doing what they should be doing instead of what men think they should be doing."

"I agree. I think she should become a doctor," I said.

"I'm glad you left the dark ages," Rachel said.

"Me too," I said.

The woman dropped us off in Lydia across the road from where the deputy sheriff had picked us up earlier.

"Hi there!"

We looked up to see Svoboda leaving a bar.

"I figured you'd be back here. So I waited to take you straight home."

From the looks of him, it seemed like he had fun waiting and quite a few beers. We got in the front seat of his car. We didn't exactly go straight home. Svoboda weaved his way back and forth, almost over the center line and almost into the ditch. It might have been better to walk home.

"Jimmie, you should play baseball this summer."

"I'm too young."

"You can run for the older men."

"I'm the slowest kid in school."

Rachel said, "I can run, and I'm a good ball player."

Svoboda said, "Don't be ridiculous. Women can't play baseball."

Rachel cringed at that comment, but she didn't say anything. Svoboda, Mr. Baseball, as they called him, was obsessed with baseball just as Rachel was obsessed with Jezebel.

She asked, "Did you ever know anyone named Jezebel who lived around here?"

"Only Jezebel I knew of was from the Bible. You should ask Jimmie's grandfather."

I wasn't sure I'd get a straight answer from my grandfather, so I asked, "Did you ever hear of anyone living in a cave?"

"Never did. It wouldn't surprise me. People settling here had to take shelter any place they could. Sometimes four families would live together in a one-room cabin until each family could build their own. I'm not that old that I would know something from back then. Again, your grandfather might know if you ask him."

It looked like I was going to have to have a talk with my grandfather.

After Svoboda dropped us off, Rachel headed home, and my uncle met me at the end of the driveway.

He said, "This envelope was in the mailbox. It's addressed to you. There was no stamp. So someone must have just thrown it in the mailbox, which is illegal, by the way. The person could be arrested for that."

I opened the letter, and I hoped the person would be arrested. It had just one line:

DON'T TELL. STOP LOOKING.

I wasn't going to tell anybody before, and I sure as hell wasn't going to now.

"What's the letter about?" my uncle asked.

"Just someone inviting me to a party."

CHAPTER 19

ROAD JUNK

Rachel and I had arranged to meet the following morning to decide our next course of action. When we had talked the night before, we realized that we had searched only a small part of the ditch. We had probably missed a lot. We needed to look through the ditch again but widen our search.

"If somebody threw something out of a passing car, it wouldn't just be in one spot," Rachel said.

"You're right. Why didn't I think of that?"

"That's why you need me around."

I sure did. I wished she would be around all the time. I knew that as soon as school started, we would be like Europe and America with an ocean between us, even though it was just the difference between a freshman and a sophomore.

"So let's meet as soon as the sun comes up. I want to get a good start in case we find anything new," I said.

"It sounds like a good idea to me."

That's why we were kicking through the ditch the next day. The weeds were still damp from dew. In a matter of minutes, our shoes and socks were soaking wet. It didn't help that we stepped into standing water along the way. After about a half hour, we still hadn't discovered anything of any value. I found an old tire and a Grain Belt beer can, of course. Why did people think they could dispose of this junk along the side of the road? There were places to toss this stuff. You needed to get gas anyway. Why not wait till you got to a gas station and throw this stuff into the trash cans put there for that purpose? By the time I got old, all the ditches would be just one giant trash heap. Did people do this in their homes? And I thought, yes, they probably did.

It would make finding what we were looking for in this ditch much easier if we didn't have to wade through all the junk. We did come upon a hairbrush. It could have come from anywhere, but it could have been Jezebel's. If only there were some way to tell from that.

I heard Rachel scream. It wasn't a scream of pain or terror but one of joy. I hurried over to her.

"I found something!"

"I figured that. What did you find?"

"Look! This looks like someone's diary. Who would throw something like this out?"

"Open it up and see if we can find out who it belongs to."

Rachel opened the diary to the first page and read aloud.

"Diary Property of: Jezebel."

"What are you doing?" Fred asked.

Rachel closed the diary quickly. We turned around to see her little brother, Snoopy, as I called him.

"What are you doing here, Fred?"

I liked my name for him better.

"Not Fred. It's Freddie. What are you doing here?" he asked.

"Just looking."

"What did you find?"

"Nothing."

"It doesn't look like nothing."

"Nothing that concerns you."

"You're my sister. So it does concern me. Do you think you're going to find the skull? It's what you've been looking for. Digging through the field and looking in the ditch. Probably looking in the cave for it. You're not going to find it."

"Why? Do you have it?" I asked.

"No. What would I be doing with a skull? I was kidding you about having a skull and burying it. I did see your grandfather throw something in the ditch. I thought you had found the skull the next day. I couldn't figure out why you were digging through the field. Looking for something that wasn't there."

Rachel said, "What are you doing up this early?"

"You made so much noise getting ready. Trying to sneak down the stairs quietly but making so much noise on those creaky steps. I decided to follow you."

"Aren't you the sneaky one!"

"Maybe I can help."

"You can help by going home."

"I'll go home. I'll tell Mom and Dad what you're up to. Hanging around with him."

"Why would it matter? Jimmie's just a boy, too young for them to be concerned," Rachel said. "Fred, go home."

Fred reluctantly left. I turned and headed to my Uncle John's house. Too young. She thought I was too young. I'd hoped she didn't think of me that way.

"Jimmie, what is the matter? Why are you walking away?"

"You think I'm too young."

"I had to tell him something. He's such a brat. Who knows what he would tell Mom and Dad? I had to tell him that."

"I know. What does it matter?" I said, "We're just trying to figure all this out."

"And we have the diary. Let's look through it."

"I'd like to look through it in private. But where?"

We looked at each other and said it at the same time.

"The cave."

CHAPTER 20

JUST PLAIN MEAN

We walked through the woods to the cave avoiding fresh cow pies. This time we took a couple of flashlights.

"I just put new batteries in," she said.

"You never can be too sure. My Uncle John says to never pass up an opportunity to use the toilet."

"I wonder what he means by that. I just go when I need to go."

"You just never know with him. He has all these sayings like that. One time, he was staring at me. I told him to stop staring at me. He said if you don't want me to stare at you, crawl in a sack, and I'll stare at the sack. That made no sense to me either. Why would he stare at a sack? These Bohemians had a lot of sayings. Like, your eyes will eat, but your stomach won't."

"Yeah, your eyes don't eat. Everyone knows that," she said.

"Like I said. These old Bohemians have all these sayings. I suppose sitting around all day without television or radio, you can come up with all sorts of things like that."

We reached the icehouse and crawled into the entrance to the cave. We turned on our flashlights and made our way through the cave to the Bohunk's room without even thinking. When we reached the room, the light from both flashlights lit up the cave. The cave, which seemed so large in the darkness and even the dim light of the candles, was actually quite small. How could that be? We were able to see things we hadn't seen before. Layers of dirt, dust, and cobwebs covered everything. Off in the corner, there was a little dresser. Why hadn't we noticed that before? We opened up one of the drawers. It was filled with men's clothes that had probably belonged to him. When we opened the bottom drawer, we expected to see more of his clothing. The drawer contained women's clothes. A couple had lived here, and when they left, they left all their clothes and belongings behind.

I said, "If this were my stuff, I'd leave it behind too."

"If it were me, I would never have had it in the first place."

"Let's read the diary."

"I'll read it to you since it's Jezebel's words," she said.

Since I liked the sound of her voice, I told her to go right ahead. I laid down on the bed, and she sat in the comfortable chair, holding her flashlight over the words of the diary.

"It starts when she was just a little girl about eight years ago. She must have been about ten."

"I could play with my dolls my whole life. My dad said I'm getting too old. He took them all away from me and burned them in the trash heap. I even had names for all of them. I don't know why he had to do that. I saw Dorothy, Belle, and Lisa burning. The black smoke rising into the air would be the last I would see of them. My dad is like that. My dad is so mean. I don't know why he does these things to me and to my mom too. Every time he goes out, he comes back angry. My mom says he has a snootful. I don't know what snootful is. It must be what happens that makes you want to beat someone up because she would get beaten and bruised. I hid under the bed. I should have done something to help her. I didn't. I was too afraid."

Rachel stopped reading.

"What could she do?" I asked. "She was only a little girl."

"It sounds like Jezebel had a mean father. It makes me glad that I have the mom and dad that I have."

"I guess we're lucky."

I had never thought of it. People said I was lucky and I just accepted it. After listening to what Rachel had read, I felt that I was really lucky.

"The whole middle part is ripped out. It's a good thing because I didn't know how much of this to read," she said. "It seems so private. Like we shouldn't be reading it. She was ten years old then. She must have been eighteen when she ran away."

"Read the rest of it. Maybe that will give us a better clue of what happened."

"You're right," she said. "The last entry is from about a year ago, July 1st, 1962. I have to leave. I can't take it anymore. I'm going to Leander's house. Leander said I could go there anytime I wanted, and he would protect me. I really needed protection. I tried locking the door. It didn't stop him from coming into my room at night. Whenever he comes into the room, I shake and tremble in fear. He comes up to the side of the bed and stares at me. He thinks I'm asleep, but I'm not. I can feel him looking at me. He just stands there and stares. That's all he does. Until this last time. He did more than look. He touched my arm, and I was really afraid. His hand moved up to my shoulder and then started to move down the front of me. I turned around quickly. Like I had a bad dream or something. He stood up and tiptoed out of the room. I know the next time, he won't stop. It just gets worse. I shouldn't have to live like this. Tomorrow, I'm going to run away. I know he will find me. It would be better if he thought I was dead. Then, he'd never look for me. Maybe I'll go see Leander. Leander is very nice. I met him at church camp last summer. He lives outside of Lakeville. He's about the same age as me. His parents died. He got the farm, and he lives there alone. He told me that he'd marry me if I wanted. I know that if I married Leander, my dad would kill him. I just hope that he can't find Leander. That he can't find me."

"Why would she throw the diary in the ditch?" I asked.

"We need to find her and make sure she's alive."

"How? We'll never find her."

"I have to know for sure," Rachel said. "What if her dad caught up with her? What if she never made it to Leander's?"

"You are a stubborn girl."

"Woman! I'm a stubborn woman. That's what you like about me."

"I guess I do."

To me, it was more like love, but like works for me.

CHAPTER 21

TOO MANY LEANDERS

We left the cave into the bright midday sun.

"How are we going to find this Leander?" I asked.

"How many Leanders can there be in Lakeville?"

"Let's check the phone book at your house."

When we got to her house, I stopped at the door. Her house was neat and clean. I wasn't sure I should go inside.

"What are you waiting for?" she asked. "Come on in."

"I'm all dirty, and your house is so clean."

"Don't be silly. We live in our house. Not show it off to people."

I followed her inside. The couch wasn't covered in plastic like our neighbor's house in New Prague. No matter what anyone said, I wasn't going to sit on that couch and get it dirty. If I needed to sit, it would be on the floor.

Her mother came in. She wore jeans and a blue work shirt. I had expected her to look like Beaver Cleaver's mom.

"You must be Jimmie. I've heard a lot about you."

"Not from Freddie, I hope."

"No, not Freddie. I don't believe much of what Freddie has to say anyway. Because what he says one day will be the total opposite the next."

Rachel said, "That's for sure. If he said the sky was blue, I wouldn't believe it even if I was looking at a blue sky."

"What brings you here today? I thought you'd never come to meet me."

"We need to look in your phone book," I said.

"Oh, you need to make a call. Feel free. Just not long distance."

"We won't be calling anybody," Rachel said.

"Why do you want to use the phone book if you're not calling someone? I know. None of my business. The phone book is right over there."

She left the room and went into the kitchen. I walked over and picked up the phone book. As I started paging through it, I realized this was going to be more difficult than I had thought. We would have to look through every page since the names were listed by last names. Some were listed with just the first initial.

Rachel said, "I don't think the phone book is going to work."

"How are we going to find this Leander? Why didn't she use the last name in her diary? That would have made it so much easier."

"Maybe Leander is the last name."

I said, "That would be too easy."

I looked at the Ls, but there was no one with the last name of Leander. Of course, it wasn't going to be that easy.

"How are we going to find this Leander in Lakeville?" I asked.

"We could go and ask around."

"We've done that before. I'm supposed to help my uncle today. Besides, I'm supposed to help him get his crop in."

Rachel said, "I have chores to do today myself."

"Maybe tomorrow. I'll ask my uncle."

"I'll ask my mom right now."

When she went into the kitchen to talk to her mom, I looked through the phone book again to see if Leander would jump out at me. If it was in there, it was going to stay in there. Rachel came out of the kitchen, with a smile on her face.

"We're in luck. She said it's okay."

"I hope my uncle says it's okay."

"Here's even better news," Rachel said, "My mom said she was planning to go to Saint Paul anyway so she can drop us off on the way and pick us up on the way back."

I hurried back to Uncle John's farm. I found him working on the seeder.

"I'm ready to help!"

"It's about time. You haven't been one lick of help since you met that girl."

"I've been busy. Do you know anybody named Leander?"

"I know a lot of Leanders."

"Would one of them be from Lakeville?"

"Sure, I believe I know a Leander from Lakeville."

Could it be this easy?

"Do you think I could meet him?"

"Why do you want to meet a ninety-year-old man in a nursing home?"

Again, it wasn't going to be that easy.

"We're just trying to find somebody is all."

"Does this have something to do with that skull? I saw you two walking through the ditch. Is this what that's all about?"

My uncle knew more about what was going on than I thought.

"Yes. The skull my grandfather threw in the weeds."

"Yeah. He told me about that. He said it was just a skull from an animal that had died in the field."

"It didn't look like that to me," I said.

"You know your grandpa's been around a while. He would know what kind of skull it was."

"I didn't get much of a chance to look at it. I wish I had, but why was it gone the next day?"

"I think you're worrying too much about nothing. Could be you're looking for an excuse to be with that girl."

"Speaking of that, we want to go to Lakeville tomorrow to find this Leander we're looking for," I said.

"Good luck with that. It may seem like a strange name to you, but Leander is a pretty popular name in that area. You're going to be looking for a needle in a haystack."

"At least we have the right haystack."

"Or you think you do," he said.

"We can't just give up. We have to find this Leander and find out what happened to Jezebel."

"Maybe you're trying to figure out a puzzle that doesn't exist. It could be something that's only in your head."

Were we making up stuff as we went along? Trying to solve a non-existent puzzle?

"By the way, here's another letter for you."

After I opened the letter and read it, I was sure this was real, and the puzzle wasn't just in my head. It was another letter of warning.

STOP LOOKING!

That wasn't going to stop me or stop us.

"If you're through reading your love letter, let's get to work. I've got a full day planned for you, and I'm going to make sure I use you."

He got that right. I had to follow the seeder around all day, making sure it wasn't plugged up and that there was enough seed in each of the bins. It saved Uncle John from stopping at the end of every row to check the bins. It was a boring job and it seemed to go on forever.

I couldn't understand how anyone would do this for a living. If it were up to me, most of the people in the world would starve. Some farmers thought it was fun. I thought it was the opposite of that. I guess that's why they called it work. After a farmer planted these seeds in the ground, he had to make sure they got enough water to grow. Once they grew, he had to cultivate in between so the weeds wouldn't take over. Then he had to hope that once they got tall enough, they weren't damaged by hail or strong winds. Or destroyed by insects. Or eaten by crows. It made me wonder how any crops ever got to be harvested.

I used the time following the seeder to search for any bones that may have belonged to the skull. I didn't see any the whole day.

A farmer's work is never done, and I believed that. Once we finished planting, we still had the farm chores to do. Milking the cows. Then feeding the cows. Cleaning the gutters. Eatings and uneatings. My dad said my uncle needed the help. So here I was. I guess I had volunteered. Volunteering for me was just being around.

It felt good to go to bed early that night. I was even too tired to eat. He made me take a few bites of something I was too tired to taste.

"Are you sure you want to go tomorrow? I think you're wasting your time."

I thought I'd been wasting my time today doing all the work on the farm, but I wasn't going to tell my uncle that. Farming was his whole life. Farming would never become mine.

CHAPTER 22

CZECH BEATLES

The following day, I walked over to Rachel's house. Rachel and her mom were already waiting for me.

"It's about time you got here."

"My uncle worked me too hard yesterday."

"You get used to it when you're a farmer," she said.

"That's not going to happen. In a few weeks, I'll be in town. That's where I'll spend the rest of my summer."

I looked at Rachel, and she seemed a little sad like she had just found out something she didn't want to hear. That I wouldn't be around all summer. Did she truly care? I wanted to think that she wanted me around, but wouldn't she rather be with someone older than I was?

Her mother said, "I have a brother who lives in town. Maybe Rachel can visit him. You can see each other once in a while throughout the summer."

Rachel said, "I'd like that."

"And you would be getting out of doing a lot of work. Like you have now."

"Yeah, like I have now."

We were on the road to Lakeville. We sat in the front seat with Rachel in the middle next to her mom, and I sat next to the window. I opened it and felt the hot air of summer blow through my hair, what little hair I had since I had a crew cut. It was getting long now. My dad would tell me it was time to get my hair cut. I hated that. I wanted to let it grow as long as the group in England called the Beatles. Their hair was long enough to cover their eyes. They played good music. Not like the polkas and waltzes you heard around here at the dance halls, but modern rock and roll that my parents and most other parents didn't like. They believe it was the work of the devil and would never last. It probably wouldn't. Polkas and waltzes have been around forever. According to my dad, this music of the Beatles would be gone in no time.

We didn't even have a record player, so I didn't have records. I heard their songs on my transistor radio, but their songs weren't played as often as "The Wanderer" or "Wolverton Mountain" on WDGY.

Some kids I knew formed bands that played around the area. They had electric guitars with amps, and they would try to sound like the Beatles. It mostly sounded like a bunch of guys singing Beatles songs with a strong Czech accent. My dad liked those Beatles songs better.

When we got to Lakeville, Rachel's mom asked where to drop us off.

Rachel said, "By that Catholic Church over there."

After we got out, I asked Rachel why we were stopping there.

"You know what we read in Jezebel's diary. She said something about meeting Leander at a church camp."

"That's right," I said.

"I was thinking we could ask around at the church and see if they had a church camp last summer and if they knew Leander."

"Yeah, if they would tell us."

"Why wouldn't they? We're just a couple of kids."

We walked into the church. It was enormous, about as big as the Catholic Church in New Prague. The interior was larger than my uncle's barn. I wonder how many bales they could hold in there.

"I see someone up front. Maybe it's the priest."

After we walked up to him, Rachel asked, "Are you the priest here?"

"Thank you, but no. I'm just a Brother."

"You're the brother of the priest?"

"No, I am a Brother. A Brother in the church is like a Sister, a nun. We help out the priest. You're not Catholic, are you?"

"I don't think I'm anything. I mean, I'm Jewish."

"That's too bad. Can I help you with something?"

"Maybe you can. Do you have church camps during the summer?"

"We don't. We have groups that meet after Mass, but we don't have church camps."

"Are there any churches here in Lakeville that do have camps?"

"Oh, we aren't allowed to associate with other churches. It is a sin."

"Don't these other churches believe in God?"

"Yes, they do."

"Then why would it be a sin to associate with them?"

"Because the Pope said so. He is the leader of our Catholic Church, the one and only true Church."

Rachel was getting into something I've always wondered about.

"These other churches. Do they think they're the only one and true church?" she asked.

"Yes, I believe they do."

"How can they all be wrong?"

"They believe a little different is the problem."

"Thank you anyway. We're sorry to have bothered you."

CHAPTER 23

WHO KNOWS

After we left the church, I asked Rachel, "Now what?"

"We're going to ask around and find another church. What's the difference between the Catholic Church and the Lutheran Church?"

I said, "The Lutherans don't believe the pope should have all this authority and that he's infallible. So they formed a new church."

"I can see why, with the pope making these fallible decisions like he does. It's like he's hogging all the people to himself. I think anything that helps you become a better person, that's the way that should be."

"You would think so, wouldn't you?"

We found the Lutheran Church. When we entered, I saw it wasn't as majestic as the Catholic Church. It was smaller and more plain. The stained-glass windows weren't as ornate. No one was in the church, but I heard a lawn mower out back. We walked out behind the church and saw a man wearing a collar pushing the mower around. After we approached him, he stopped and turned off the mower.

Rachel said, "Maybe you can help us."

"You could help me by mowing the lawn, but I couldn't ask you that."

"We're looking for somebody."

"Are you looking for God?"

"No."

"That's too bad," he said.

Rachel said, "I think God is everywhere, not just in a church."

"You got me there, girl."

"Do you hold camps in the summer?"

"Yes, would you like to attend one?"

"No, we're asking about one from last summer."

"What about it?"

"We asked because we're looking for someone from around here who went to one of those camps. We're looking for a girl who disappeared. She mentioned Leander. Was there a Leander who went to your church camp?"

"I can't say."

"Who can say?"

"Only Leander."

"How can he tell us if we can't find him?" I asked.

"Did you ever think he might not want to be found?" he asked.

"Why not? Did he do something wrong?"

"Sometimes people who do nothing wrong still don't want to be found by people looking for them."

Rachel said, "If someone were looking for me, I would want them to know I was okay. It's just that we want to help this girl, Jezebel. Leander might know where she is."

His eyebrows raised a bit, and then he looked away.

"I can't help you."

He started up the mower. Just like the period at the end of a sentence, that was the end of the conversation.

"I think we have the right church and the right camp," I said. "Did you see the look on his face when we mentioned Leander and Jezebel?"

"Yes. It seemed like he knew who they were."

"So how are we going to find them?"

CHAPTER 24

COCA-COLA SILO

Rachel said, "I know one thing. Kids around here who are their age and went to that camp probably wouldn't worry about talking about Leander and Jezebel like the minister and brother did."

"How will we find out which kids went to the camp?"

"I say we go to the soda fountain at the drugstore and ask around there. There's bound to be some kids about our age or Jezebel's age, we could ask."

"You know, Rachel, I can tell you're a sophomore, and I'm a freshman. You're so much smarter than I am. I couldn't think like that."

"I'll always be smarter than you. Just remember that."

We headed down the street to the central part of the town and found the Rexall Drugstore. After we walked inside, I felt the air-conditioning. I didn't realize how hot I was, even though it was hotter yesterday at Uncle John's farm.

"Do you have any money, Jimmie?"

"I have a couple of dollars."

"We can buy a lot of stuff in here for that. You don't mind buying, do you?"

"What I have, you're welcome to."

I would buy her anything if I could. All she had to do was ask. That's if I had the money.

"Let's each get a malt. I like strawberry malts," she said.

"I do too."

We had so much in common, but maybe everybody liked strawberry malts. We walked in. I noticed that most people there were very old. They wouldn't know about Leander or Jezebel or a church camp. If they did, why would they tell us?

We walked up to the counter and ordered our malts. The soda jerk looked to be about my age and seemed bored. He was red-faced with acne all over his face.

After he brought over the malts, I asked, "Can you help me?"

"I just did."

"Do you go to church?"

"That's a hell of a question!"

Rachel was much better at this than I was. "He means, do you go to the Lutheran Church?"

"No, I go to the Catholic Church. What's it to you?"

He wasn't going to be any help. Just then, a group of girls about Rachel's age walked in. They sat down at a booth.

"Let me handle this," she said.

She got no argument from me.

We walked over and sat at a table next to them. I listened to them. They were talking about boys. Which boys they'd like to go out with and which boys they wouldn't. I probably was one of the boys in the wouldn't group. That's the kind of girls they were. My being with Rachel maybe made me seem that much more attractive. They kept glancing over at me.

Rachel got up and went up to the group.

"Hello. I'm new in town, and I'm looking for a church. I was wondering if they had any church camps in the summer."

Three of them immediately said they didn't know. But one girl said, "Yeah. I know of one."

"Which one is that?"

"It's the church down the road."

"Is the church camp any good?"

"I went there last year. It was pretty good. Some religious talk but not too much. At least it got me away from my stupid brother."

"That's what I need. Something to get me away from my stupid little brother. I guess everyone's got one of those."

The girls looked at me and giggled.

"Oh, not him. This is my friend, Jimmie."

The girls said in unison, "Hi, Jimmie."

Before I could answer, Rachel said, "A friend of mine went to a church camp here last year. Her name is Jezebel. Maybe you remember her from camp."

The girl's eyes lit up when she heard the name Jezebel.

"I know who she is. She had a friend named Leander who was at the camp."

"I'd like to meet up with them and maybe go to camp with them again this summer. That's if they're going. How do I find this Leander?"

"He's got a farm about three miles out of town. His folks left it to him."

Both Rachel and I knew we had hit upon the right Leander.

"Can you tell us how to get there?" I asked, surprising myself.

"Just take that highway there," she said, pointing. "You can't miss it. The silo is painted like a giant Coca-Cola can."

She pointed to the Coca-Cola sign above the soda fountain as if I had never seen one before.

"Thank you," I said. "You've been a great help. Are you going to the camp this summer?"

What had gotten into me? Asking all these questions to a girl I didn't even know.

"No, we're going to Disneyland."

There's Disneyland again. I'll probably never get to go there, and yet another person is going.

"Well, have fun at Disneyland," I said.

Rachel had had enough. She grabbed my arm and dragged me out of the drugstore.

"I wasn't finished with my malt!"

"You could have been if you hadn't been so busy talking."

"I was just trying to help."

CHAPTER 25

THE LONG WALK

Rachel and I stood outside the drugstore planning our next move.

"How do you feel about walking three miles?" Rachel asked.

"We could try hitchhiking again."

"Nope. My mom warned me about hitchhiking the other day. Svoboda must have talked to her and told her what we were doing. She told me never to hitchhike again."

"But she's not here."

She pointed a finger to her head. "No, she's up here. And that's the worst place for her to be when I want to do something like this."

"So walking it is."

"Yeah, walking it is."

We headed out of town on the highway the girl had mentioned. It was a hot day, and I realized we should have gotten water. A half mile down the road, we were both thirsty. We walked off the highway toward a farmhouse. A hose was attached to a faucet sticking out of the side of the house.

"I'm so thirsty, I could drink out of that horse trough over there," Rachel said.

"I've done it many times, and I survived. Let's drink out of that hose."

"My mom said drinking from a hose can make you sick."

"I think walking along a hot road and not drinking water would make me sick. I'll go first."

When she turned on the water, it came out warm. I waited for the water to cool and then gulped down as much as I could. I handed the hose to her, and she started drinking. A man appeared from behind the house.

"What the hell are you doing here?"

"We were walking down the road, and we needed some water."

"You should have asked."

"We didn't see anybody."

"All you had to do is knock on the door, but since you're already drinking, go right ahead. Where are you two going?"

"We're heading down the road," Rachel said. "We're looking for Leander's farm."

"You could be walking a while because I don't know any Leander around here. But I'm new to the area. If you're out walking in this heat, you need to take some water with you."

He rinsed out a couple of milk bottles that looked reasonably clean and filled each of them with water.

"Now, carry these along with you. I don't want to see you two dying along the side of the road."

"We don't either," I said.

He chuckled at that, "You two have a good day. I got work to do. Not that either of you would know about work."

I said, "I helped my uncle plant corn yesterday."

"Kind of late, isn't it?"

"I don't know. My uncle figured it was okay."

"It'll never be knee-high by the Fourth of July," he said. "You'll be lucky if it's knee-high by Labor Day."

"My uncle knows things."

"Seems like you just wasted some good seed, if you ask me."

He turned without saying goodbye, hitched up his overalls, and walked into the barn. We walked out onto the road, each carrying our bottles of water.

Rachel said, "That was very nice of him."

"I guess people can be nice if you give them a chance. It's the mean ones you got to watch out for."

We got onto the road and continued walking. The sun was a little higher in the sky, so it must have been almost noon. We were only about two miles out of town. The jugs of water were nearly empty, and we still hadn't seen the Coca-Cola silo. We passed over a hill and came to a stop sign. We had reached the end of the road as it came to a T.

"I hate it when I get directions, and they say I can't miss it. I always miss it," I said.

"I've heard that before. How could we miss it?"

"Maybe Leander repainted the silo."

"What do you think? Left or right?" she asked.

"I think neither. She said it was right on this road."

"There's a house over there. A woman is outside, sitting in a chair and reading a book. Let's ask her."

When we approached the woman, she said, "My goodness. What are you two doing wandering around in the middle of nowhere?"

"We're looking for Leander's house," I said.

"I'm sorry. I don't know any Leander around here."

"We're looking for a farm with a silo painted like a Coca-Cola can."

"I don't know of any silo like that on any of the roads around here, and I've been here all my life. Whoever told you this must have been mistaken."

"She sounded pretty sure it was on this road from Lakeville."

"Did she tell you to take the east road out of town or west?"

"She pointed to go down this road."

"Maybe she was turned around. She probably should have been pointing in the other direction because this road also heads the other direction out of Lakeville."

"You're probably right," Rachel said. "Sorry to have disturbed you."

"You two look quite thirsty. Can I get you each a glass of lemonade?"

I said, "That sounds good to us."

She went in. We sat on one of her benches. A few minutes later, she came out and handed us each a glass of lemonade. I took a gulp, and I wished I hadn't done it. It was the worst-tasting lemonade I had ever had in my life. The sour look on my face probably matched the sour taste of the lemonade. I looked over at Rachel, who had just taken a sip. She looked over at me, away from the woman. She also had a sour look on her face. How could we refuse to drink her lemonade?

I said, "We each have these jars. How about if we pour the lemonade in them and then we'll have something to drink along the way?"

"That sure is smart of you. You'll go a long way in this world."

"I don't want to go a long way. I just want to go to Lakeville," I said.

"Head in that direction," she said as she pointed.

"I hope you're pointing in the right direction."

She laughed, "Yes, that's the way. You take care now."

CHAPTER 26
FIFTY CENTS WASTED

We got on to the road and headed back from where we had come. A car stopped for us about a half mile away and asked if we wanted a ride. I was tempted, but Rachel shook her head no. Her mother's voice was in her head telling her not to. So her mother's voice was in my head telling me the same thing.

"We're just out for a walk," I said.

He took off, shaking his head, not understanding why two people would rather walk than ride in a car on a hot day like this. We reached the farm where we had gotten the jugs of water. When we left the woman's farm, we emptied the lemonade onto her lawn. I hoped it wouldn't kill her grass. We should have poured it on some weeds instead. The farmer saw us and waved us over.

He said, "You're back again."

"That woman down the road gave us some lemonade, but we're sure thirsty. Could you spare some more water?"

"You mean Mrs. Grayson. I've had some of her lemonade. It's going to take you a month to get rid of that taste!"

I figured it might take me longer. I might never drink lemonade again.

When we got to Lakeville, we went into the drugstore and ordered two more malts to see if we could get the taste of that lemonade out of our mouths. The girls weren't at the booth. I don't know if the girl knew what she had done or if it was just a mistake that she sent us off in the wrong direction. If it was intentional, it was quite a mean trick.

The farmer was right. The malted milk didn't get rid of the taste of that lemonade. It was fifty cents wasted as far as I could see.

"How much time do we have before your mom gets back?"

"A couple of hours."

"Think we can find that place and get back in time?"

"We can try."

"What if we're not here when she gets here?"

"She'll have to wait, but she won't be happy. I don't want to see her after she's had to wait for a while. We'd better go."

When we asked the same kid behind the counter to fill up our jugs with water, he acted as if we were stealing from him. We spent money there. It's not like the water cost him anything.

We left the store and headed out of town in the other direction. Soon, we were in the country and saw farmers hard at work in the field cultivating. They were ahead of the game, as my dad would say. I saw rows of little corn seedlings peeking out of the ground.

As we walked along, cars stopped for us again. Each time Rachel said no.

A young man with a beard and dressed in bibber overalls stopped and offered us a ride. When Rachel refused, he got quite angry and swore at us.

"The hell with you! Don't take my damn ride then."

Rachel tried apologizing, telling him her mom said she shouldn't take rides from anybody.

"Yeah, right. The hell with you!"

We walked almost two miles and still hadn't seen a farm with a Coca-Cola silo.

Rachel said, "I think that girl was just pulling our leg. I don't think there is any farm with a silo like that."

"She seemed nice enough. She went to a church camp and everything."

"We don't know if she went to a church camp. She could have been lying about that. She could be like my brother who lies about everything."

"Yeah, you're right. It's the only thing we have to go on now."

When we reached the top of the next hill, I could see the top of a silo. It was painted red and white near the top.

"Hey!" Rachel said. "There it is. Up ahead."

"Yeah, that must be Leander's place."

CHAPTER 27

NONE OF YOUR BUSINESS

We picked up our pace and walked faster just in case the Coca-Cola silo decided to disappear on us. We reached the driveway and took a left down a narrow-rutted road. His farmhouse was freshly painted. It seemed like the lawn was well cared for.

When we reached the house, we walked onto the porch and knocked on the door. There was no answer. Rachel knocked again, this time louder. There was still no answer. We hadn't considered that he might not be home, but I guess we had to try.

"Let's just sit and wait a little while and still be back in town in time for my mom."

After about five minutes, we heard a pickup coming out of the back fields. It looked like the pickup that belonged to the guy who swore at us earlier. He stopped when he saw us on the porch.

"So I'm not good enough for a ride, but I'm good enough for you to sit on my porch."

Rachel gave him her cutest smile.

"I'm sorry. We're looking for somebody."

"Aren't we all?"

"We're looking for Leander. Would you know where he is?" she asked.

"Sure, I know where he is. You're looking at him. Why would you be looking for me?"

If Jezebel had gone to this guy, she must have been desperate. I don't know what Rachel thought of him, but I didn't think he was worth the time of day, let alone coming to him for help. I guess if you're desperate, you'll do anything.

I asked, "Did you go to a church camp last summer?"

"What's it to you?"

"We're just wondering. We're looking for a girl named Jezebel, and we think maybe she might have come to see you."

"Why are you looking for her?"

"We're just trying to find out where she went," Rachel said.

"Yeah, you and a lot of other people. As I told them, I haven't seen her. I don't know anything about where she went."

"You mean other people have been asking about her?"

"Damn right. I don't think everyone should have their nose in someone else's business. I think Jezebel would rather be left alone. Don't you?"

I said, "Didn't Jesus preach to help your neighbor? We're just trying to help our neighbor, Jezebel. We're all children of God."

Where was I getting this from? His mood softened a bit.

"It seems like you're religious people. A lot more than the last ones that came here. So I'm going to try to help you. The best help I can tell you is to leave Jezebel alone. If she left that father of hers, she left for good reason. That's all I'm going to say on this. Now, if you want to get back to town, I'll give you a ride. That's if your mother would think it's all right to take a ride from me."

"Rachel, do you think it'd be all right?"

Rachel thought for a few seconds. "Yeah, I guess it is. We do have to get back into town to meet my mother when she returns from Saint Paul."

This time, Rachel put me in between Leander and herself. She sat near the window. If something was going to happen, it would happen to me and not her. I guess that was okay by me.

We got into town, and Leander dropped us off at the drugstore. Her mom wasn't there yet. We sat outside on a bench, watching traffic pass by.

"What do you think?" I asked. "Jezebel's not here."

"While you were busy looking at other things at the farm, I looked in the window. Women's things were inside. A woman's suit and a pink suitcase. Short dresses. I don't think Leander wears dresses."

"Could be his mother's."

"They didn't look like a mother's kind of dress. It looked like a dress someone named Jezebel would wear."

"You think she's staying there?" I asked.

"Yes, I do. Leander did his best to get rid of us."

"Did it work?"

"No way."

"Don't tell me we're going to walk back there again."

"No. When my mom gets here, I'll ask her to go out there with us. We might have better luck if she's along."

CHAPTER 28

SORRY TO BOTHER YOU

Half an hour and two more malts later, Rachel's mom pulled up in front of the Rexall Drugstore. We went out to meet her. Rachel got into the car, and I followed her into the passenger seat again.

"Mom. Can I ask you a favor?"

"Another one? It's been a long day, and I'm anxious to get home."

"We've found Leander, but he says he doesn't know anything about Jezebel. I think she's there, and if you went along with us, he might say something about where she is."

"You want me to drive out there?"

"If you would, Mom. Please."

"Since you asked so nicely, that's what we'll do."

We crested the hill and saw the Coca-Cola silo. I saw Leander's pickup in front. We pulled into the driveway and parked behind the pickup. Leander came out of the house with the 'now what' look on his face. When he saw Rachel and me, he lifted his hands in the air. But when he saw Rachel's mom, he waved us up onto the porch. He took a seat.

"Leander. This is my mother."

Rachel's mom said, "We're sorry to bother you. My kids are insistent about finding Jezebel, and they figure you must know something about where she is."

"I don't," he said. "Just like I told them."

Rachel's mom was more insistent.

"Is there anything you can tell us about where Jezebel might be?"

"I have no idea. She was supposed to come here, and she never showed up. That's all I know."

"Do you know anybody from that Lutheran camp who might know where she is?" Rachel asked.

"Lutheran camp? What would we be doing at a Lutheran camp? It was the Catholic Church that had a camp. That's where I met Jezebel.

"How come she went to a Catholic church camp way out here so far from home?"

"I was a good friend of her brother, and he went to this camp. That's how I got to know Jezzy."

"Maybe he knows where she is and went to see him," Rachel said.

"Shortly after camp, he went into the Marines, and he wasn't there more than a few weeks when he got killed by a sniper. I lost my mom and my best friend all in a matter of weeks."

"We're so sorry to hear that," Rachel's mom said.

"Why didn't the brother at the church tell us about the church camp?" Rachel asked.

"You must mean Brother Thomas? He's a weird duck. He wanted to be a priest, but he had a lot of problems, and the only thing he was suited for was to serve as a brother. You can't take anything he says as fact."

"Like my brother, Freddie."

"I don't know about him, but I know about Brother Thomas. I think you should see Father Arthur. He and Jezzy were quite close at the camp."

Before we left, Rachel had to ask another question.

"Who belongs to those dresses in your house? They don't look like something your mother would wear."

"They belong to my girlfriend if you must know. Now get the hell off my property!"

I guess it was one question too many.

CHAPTER 29

THE FATHER ARTHUR SANDWICH

We left Leander's farm toward home. It had been a long day. I was surprised I wasn't tired. That could have been because we were getting closer to finding out what happened to Jezebel.

"Can I ask you one more favor, Mom?"

"I know. You want to go see Father Arthur."

"Yes. If you would. Please."

"Anything for you. You are my master. I guess you do help a lot around the farm, but you're going to help a little bit more because you'll have extra chores tonight."

"That's okay, it'll be worth it. I just want to talk to Father Arthur."

"So do I, dear. So do I."

We pulled up to the Catholic church again and started walking into the church.

Rachel's mom stopped us. "No. This way. We'll go to the rectory. That's where we might find him."

We knocked on the door. Nobody answered. We rang the doorbell. Finally, a woman came out. She had a dust rag in her hand and carried a broom.

"Can I help you?"

Rachel's mom answered, "We'd like to see Father Arthur."

"You're not one of the parishioners."

"No, we just have a question for him."

"He's pretty busy, but I'll go check to see if he'll see you."

We waited a few minutes until a white-haired priest turned the corner. He walked with a limp and used a cane.

He approached us and asked, "Can I help you?"

"Yes, I'm sorry to disturb you, but my two young ones here are looking for someone. We think you might be able to help. Someone by the name of Jezebel."

From the look on his face, I could tell that he knew Jezebel.

"Sorry, I can't help you."

"Rachel and Jimmie here found her purse with a picture and a diary in the ditch. They'd like to return it. I think Jezebel would be interested in having it back."

"I'm sorry, but I don't think I can help you."

Rachel's mom said, "You know where she is, don't you?"

"If I did, and I'm not saying I do, I'm not at liberty to say."

"How about this? I'll give you our name and phone number. She can call us if she's interested. That's if you know where she is. If not, you can throw this away."

Father Arthur seemed like he was sandwiched. Put in between two pieces of bread, and neither of them tasted good.

Rachel's mom turned to leave.

"I'm sorry to have taken up your time. Have a good day."

"Wait a second," he said. "You're much nicer than her father. He came to see me twice asking about Jezebel. When he said Jezebel was his daughter, I let him know where she was. I know now I shouldn't have. I didn't want to make that mistake again."

"They just want to know she's okay. Any information you can give us would be appreciated."

"I can't tell you where she is, but I can tell you this. She is with God."

"You mean she's dead," Rachel said.

"No, no. That isn't what I mean. She is safe in another town. She has decided to enter the convent. She has received the calling to become a nun and serve our Lord."

CHAPTER 30

THE CALLING

When we returned to the farm, Rachel and I stood at the end of her driveway. Shep spotted us and ran over from my uncle's place. The sun was about to set in the west over Tupa's farm. I'd never stopped to watch a sunset before. With Rachel next to me, it seemed like the right thing to do.

"Now what?" she asked.

I wasn't sure what she meant. Was there something we were supposed to do when watching a sunset? If there was, I didn't know what it was.

"About what?"

"We know Jezebel is safe and happy. As happy as she can be. Not that becoming a nun is safe."

"She's safer now than when she was living with her dad."

"It seems like sort of a drastic measure, though. Don't you think?"

"It's because she had a calling," I said.

"I guess if you have the calling, you must answer it."

"What would you do if you had the calling?"

"I would never become a nun."

"That's right. You aren't even Catholic."

"There is that. Plus I don't think I'd look good in their habits."

I thought she would look good in anything she wore, but I wasn't sure if I should tell her that.

"You'd have to go to Mass every day," I said. "And all the time they spend praying. In the Catholic school, we went to Mass every day. I've been to church so many times; it should last me for the rest of my life. If you're praying and going to Mass all the time, at least you aren't going to get in any trouble."

"I'd probably find a way."

"What are we going to do about the skull?"

"Are you sure it even was a skull?" Rachel asked.

"Yes, I'm sure of it. I saw it."

"We should forget about it. It's something we'll never know the answer to."

"I suppose you're right. Besides, my uncle has finished using me, and it looks like I'll be going back to town tomorrow."

"I think you should spend the whole summer here and play baseball with Joe Svoboda."

I felt glad that she wanted me around longer. Maybe that was because there was no one else around.

"That would mean I might have to work."

"Would that be so bad?"

It would be a chance to be around Rachel. That's something that sounded good to me.

"I think we should explore that cave some more," Rachel said. "We need to find the skull. Let's take Shep along."

I needed to spend more time with Shep. I had been ignoring her and spending all my time with Rachel. I was afraid she might start to get jealous of Rachel. I didn't think so because Shep seemed to like her. Shep went up to her and nuzzled her leg. When Rachel bent down, Shep licked her face. Rachel didn't mind. Some girls in town would have pushed Shep away.

CHAPTER 31

TOO MANY NOTES

The following day, I sat at the end of my uncle's driveway, waiting for Rachel. Instead, I saw Freddie, the last person I wanted to see. He came up and sat by me.

"What are you doing?" he asked.

"Waiting for your sister. If you helped her with her chores, she could have done them sooner."

"She didn't help me. So why should I help her?"

"I guess that's one way of looking at it."

"You two have been hanging around a lot together."

"I'm still trying to figure out what happened to that skull."

"That skull is gone."

"You said it was a skull from school."

"I was mistaken about that."

That meant he was lying about it being a skull from school, but he wouldn't admit it. Was he lying about finding the skull in the ditch too?

"Can I hang around with you two today?"

I didn't want him to, but I couldn't think of any way to get rid of him. We watched a couple of cars pass by in each direction. After Joe Svoboda turned into his driveway, I saw Rachel walking down the ditch. I walked toward her, with Freddie following close behind. She saw me and said, "I found one. It's for your uncle."

"Who is it from?"

"From the Social Security."

"Oh, good. It's what he's been waiting for."

"So he's been missing some letters as well."

"Yes. Let's walk in the other ditch back toward my uncle's place."

As we walked in that ditch, Freddie followed behind, listening to every word we said. We had to be careful of what we were talking about. Not that we talked about anything to be careful about. Ever. But he must have thought so.

"I found one," Freddie said as he held up a letter.

"Who's it for?" Rachel asked.

"I found it. It's mine. Didn't you ever hear the rule - finders keepers, losers weepers?"

"Give me the letter or I'll…"

Freddie handed the letter to Rachel before she could finish the threat. I saw it was another letter for Uncle John. He might not be happy to hear about this one because it looked like a bill.

"Who cares about some stupid old letters?" Freddie asked.

"Some people have been taking letters and tossing them in the ditch."

"What happens if they get caught?"

"They get fined a hundred dollars and maybe spend a month in jail."

I didn't know for sure, but in case he was thinking of it, I wanted to make sure he knew there was some penalty involved for doing that.

Freddie handed a letter to me.

"Oh, yeah. I found another letter earlier. It's for you."

It was addressed in big, plain handwriting. There was no postmark. I opened the letter and looked inside. It said in huge letters,

IF YOU CARE ABOUT SHEP, STOP LOOKING!

"They wouldn't hurt her, would they?" I asked.

"Nobody could be that mean," Rachel said.

"I hope not."

"Stop looking for what?" Freddie said.

"It could be the skull, but they never mentioned it. If it was Jezebel, she would tell us to stop looking for her. Don't you think? If she entered a convent, why would she care if we found her?" she asked.

"I know one thing. I'm keeping Shep close to me from now on. But I'm going to keep on looking."

"I am too."

And Freddie said, "I am too."

Oh great. We'll never be rid of the little kid.

Freddie handed another envelope to me. I saw it was addressed to me, but it had no postmark or stamp.

"Where'd you get this letter?" I asked.

"I found it in the ditch. Just now."

It looked like it hadn't been in the weeds too long. I opened it and pulled out a letter. It contained a message in letters cut out from a magazine.

STOP LOOKING OR ELSE!

"Another one of these," I said.

"Let me see that," Rachel said.

She looked at the letter closely. Then she looked at Freddie.

"Okay. I know what you're up to."

"I didn't do anything."

"I emptied the trash yesterday. I saw cut-up magazines. I bet you if I looked, these letters were cut out from them. You made this letter, didn't you?"

Freddie looked a little sheepish, nodded, and said, "Yes."

"And the other letters?"

"No. Just this one."

"And what about the letters in the ditch? Did you take them out of the mailbox?"

"You don't get it, do you, Rach? It's boring out here. I had to think of some fun stuff to do, and this seemed like fun."

"Like we told you, Freddie," I said. "It's against the law. I have half a mind to turn you in."

"You don't even have half a mind."

"Freddie!" Rachel said. "That'll be enough!"

I said, "I've got another question. You found that skull in the ditch, didn't you?"

"Uh, yes, I did. I knew you were looking for it. I thought it'd be a good trick to see you looking and looking, and it was. I laughed every time you walked around in this ditch."

"Okay, where is the skull?"

"I don't know if I should tell you."

"Tell us, or I'll go to Mom about these letters."

"Okay. I found that skull. The next day, before I first talked to you, I hid it in the cave."

"You knew about the cave?"

"I found that the first day I was here. Like I said, I was bored. I had to hurry because your dog was following me. I've never run so fast. I ran into the cave and hid that skull right in plain sight. In that room with the bed and the chair. You didn't look close enough. I'm surprised you didn't see it right away."

Rachel said, "It was too dark in there to see anything."

"I have to ask. Did you trap us in there? Twice?"

"Yes. I thought that was funny too. I wouldn't have left you in there. I'd have gotten you out. I could hear you in there. Boy, I had a laugh at that one."

"You get on home, Freddie," Rachel said. "Before I do something you'll be sorry for."

"Yeah. Yeah," he said as he turned and left for home.

Rachel said, "We're going into the cave. But tomorrow. It's too late today."

The following day, we grabbed our flashlights and headed for the cave. When we reached the icehouse, the sun had just risen. We entered through the opening in the back of the icehouse. On our way to the Bohunk's room, we took a wrong turn and came to the tunnel with the drawings on the walls.

"You know," I said. "I bet you Freddie did these drawings too."

"Maybe. It kind of looks like his stupid artwork."

"I don't know what you're going to do with a brother like that."

"I have to put up with him. He's the only one I've got."

We found the Bohunk's room and searched for the skull. Then, we saw it way back in a far corner. He said he hid it in plain sight, but only the top could be seen behind some books.

"We've got the skull. Now what do we do with it?" I asked.

"We turn it over to the sheriff. Let him figure it out."

Then, I saw the journal hidden behind the skull.

"Look. Here's the journal I found before my candle went out. Freddie must have hidden it there."

"I wonder what it says."

She got on the bed, and I sat in the chair. I opened the journal and started reading to her.

PART TWO: THE JOURNAL - 1875

CHAPTER 32

BOHEMIA

I was eighteen years old and not afraid of many things.

Even with my eyes wide open, I could see only blackness darker than night. I had expected that. That wasn't what bothered me. Because of where I was, I couldn't move. I was jammed inside a barrel on board a wagon headed out of Bohemia, a barrel that was last used for pickles. The smell of them was overwhelming. I would never eat another pickle again. I had been rocked, rolled, shaken, and dropped.

It seemed like almost everyone in Bohemia was after me. I did have a passport, but I didn't have permission to leave my village. The landlords not only took most of the money earned from the crops we raised but also prevented us from moving to neighboring towns, let alone another country. There was also the matter of an angry ex-fiancé, her parents, her four brothers, my angry parents, and my sisters and brothers. Our parents had arranged the marriage and I wasn't too happy with the arrangement. This was my only means of escape.

My jug of water, once full, contained only a few drops. I had rationed the water but had no way to determine how much time had elapsed between drinks. I had sweated most of it out, which explained why I didn't have to urinate, thankfully.

I hoped America in 1875 would be better than Bohemia. Bohemia didn't approve of anyone who didn't believe as everyone else did. There had to be a place for a free thinker in the world. I had heard America was such a place.

I had received a letter from my brother in Minnesota which had affordable land. Land which was much like that in Bohemia. There was also a town named Nova Praha after our city in Bohemia. Some villages were populated with immigrants from my homeland. To prepare, I had learned to speak English from a cousin who had returned from New York.

After what seemed like months, someone opened the barrel. I had arrived.

"Finally! New York!" I said.

"New York? Hell, we only crossed the border between Bohemia and Germany half a day ago!"

Some people had no sense of humor.

My journey had just begun.

CHAPTER 33

THE AUSTRIAN

At least now, I no longer needed to hide in the barrel. The Germans weren't chasing me. They didn't care about an insignificant Czech. I crawled out of the barrel, unable to stand up straight. I couldn't move my legs, and when I did, I wished I hadn't. I almost passed out from the pain.

A man came over to help. Compared to his fancy suit and vest, my worn-out shoes, work pants, and dirty shirt looked even worse for the wear. Even the suit coat I wore didn't improve my appearance. He eyed me through his monocle.

"Are you okay?" the man asked in German. Fortunately, I understood some German, as some spoke it in our village. The man had a white goatee and seemed quite old, much older than my deceased grandfather. I was surprised the man could still be alive.

"I'm fine," I said in half German and half Czech.

"Would you like some water?"

"I'd like some beer."

"Beer. You must be Czech," he laughed.

We walked across the street and found a table in a dark corner of a tavern. Over a few beers, he told me he was Austrian, and I told him of my plan to emigrate to America.

The Austrian said, "Even after days in that barrel, you still smile."

"I never stop. One of my nicknames back home is Smiley. Or Smajlik as they would say."

"It's good you have a passport to travel."

"Yes, I have that," I said.

"And you do have permission from your landlord to leave, right?"

"Of course, I do," I lied, not sure I should trust the Austrian.

"That's good. They don't let just anyone go to America."

My spirits sank as I envisioned ships leaving for America without me.

"But do you have the money for passage?" he asked. "It costs a lot of money for an ocean voyage."

"Yes. I have money."

I patted my coat above where I had hidden my hard-earned cash.

"That is good. With money, anything is possible. Let me buy you a beer and a Slivovitz."

Slivovitz is a fruit brandy. I had developed a taste for it. Too much of a taste.

One beer led to another. One Slivovitz led to another. My Austrian friend put it on his bill. He told me to save my money. I would need it when I got to America.

"If I didn't have a wife and children, I would embark on this adventure with you."

"That's too bad. Having a companion like you with me on this voyage would be helpful."

He waved to the bartender.

"Another round for my Czech friend here! Put it on my tab!"

I closed my eyes for a second, it seemed. But it must have been longer since it was now dark outside. My friendly Austrian host was gone.

I asked the bartender, "Did he go to the toilet?"

"No. He left."

"He went home?"

"Home? He has no home here. I've never seen him before."

"Then where did he go?"

"All I know is he said that now that he had money, he was going to America."

Now that he had money!? But he was buying all the drinks. Unless? I reached inside my coat. I shouldn't have trusted the Austrian. My money was gone!

CHAPTER 34

A STUPID BOHUNK

"You'll never catch up to him. He's probably throwing up on the ship right now," the bartender said.

"What can I do? I need to get to America."

He said, "You'll need money. To get money, you'll have to work. Or you'll need to trick some stupid Bohunk out of his money. Maybe get him drunk and steal it."

I said, "I can't do that. I know a Bohunk has to work hard for money."

"There you go then; you'll have to work. You need to pay me for all the drinks."

"But the Austrian paid."

"Like hell. I need someone here in my tavern to help me. You say you are honest. I believe you when you say you wouldn't cheat someone. After you work off your debt, I might hire you to help me in the bar here. You can pour beer, can't you?"

"Yes, as easy as I can drink it."

"As long as you pour it and don't drink it. Uh, you do know how to handle money?"

"Yes. Tell me what you charge for beers."

"More than our customers can afford. It's written down next to the cash drawer."

"Do you serve anything else besides beer?"

"Don't you remember? Slivovitz. Which you've had enough of. Plenty enough of," he said.

"I know how to pour that too. And drink it."

"But in between, I want you to keep this place clean. Sweep up. Wipe the bar off. Clean out the toilets."

"Clean out the toilets?"

"Yeah. Drunks here aren't so neat in the bar, but when they get to the toilet, they are worse. They are like pigs in a sty. When you go in there, you'll see that I try to keep it reasonably clean. I would like you to do the same."

I walked in, and the odor greeted me like a slap in the face. Men pissed along the side of a wall I don't think had ever been cleaned. There was no place to wash hands, but there was a dirty old towel that hung from a rack.

"Don't you have any clean towels?"

"That is the clean towel."

"The first thing I'll do is wash it."

"Why wash it? They will just dirty it up anyway."

I went out to the bar.

"Here's your first customer. Wait on him, and I'll see how you do."

"Who the hell are you?" the customer asked.

"Who the hell are you?" I asked.

"The same man as I was yesterday. I'm Franz, from town. Everyone knows me."

"Well, I don't know you."

"You're not from town, are you? How come you are here instead of Ivan."

"He hired me to tend the bar to pay off my debt."

"Good Lord. He finally found a sucker to work for him, huh? He is the meanest boss around. He'll work you from when you get up in the morning until you go to sleep at night. You'll be lucky if he even pays you."

I said, "I guess I'll be lucky too if I even have food at the end of the day and a place to sleep, and that's what he has promised me."

"Or if you can live through his cooking. If you can, you can live through anything, I guess. So where's my beer?"

There were several different taps alongside the bar.

"Just one question. Which beer do you drink?" I asked.

"The same as always."

Bartending was going to be more difficult than I had thought it would be.

"I don't know which beer that is."

"What other beer would any self-respecting German drink?" He pointed to the tap. "That one. The cheapest. When my friends come, they drink the same thing."

I poured him a glass. He scowled.

"That little glass? You see that mug up there above you? That is my stein. I drink out of it every time I come here. My father drank out of that. And my father's father. My son will drink out of it after I'm gone. But now I am drinking out of it. If you will pour me a beer."

"You've lived here all your life?"

"Yes, where else would I live?"

"America. Like where I want to live."

"Don't we all. How are you getting there?" he asked.

"That's just it. I have no money."

"You have a passport to get out?"

"Yes," I said. "But I need to make it to the ship before the passport expires, and I need to make enough money to pay for my voyage."

"You'll have to work an eternity here to earn that much money."

"Maybe there is some other way I can make money."

"Without cheating someone? Good luck with that. How about if we do this? You can come out to my sawmill and help me cut up logs. We cut the logs here for most houses. Perhaps I could use your help."

I said, "That work I would like better than pouring beer and cleaning toilets."

"I'm sure. You'd make more money too," he said.

I wanted to quit my bartending job five minutes after I had gotten it.

"I need to find out something."

I walked up to Ivan and asked, "When would I have to work here?"

"We need somebody at night. I can be here during the day."

"Perfect."

I returned to Franz and said, "I can work for you. But I have to be done by six."

"You'll be done by four. I need two hours of drinking before I go home to my wife."

"Four o'clock, it is."

I walked back to Ivan.

"I can start at four. If I have two jobs, I can make even more money and be on my way to America."

I tended the bar until two in the morning. I kept getting orders wrong.

"You'll get better in time."

"I'm glad you think so."

I arrived at the sawmill early the next day. My job was to grab boards off the giant blade and stack the heavy wet boards. After fifteen minutes, my hands were bleeding and raw.

"Do you have gloves?"

"I don't need gloves," Franz said.

"I do."

"Then you should have brought some along."

After half an hour, my hands were swollen, sweaty, and sore. I pulled a board off the blade. It slipped out of my hand into the blade and flew back, almost taking Franz's head off.

"I don't think I can use you," he said.

I was fired after only thirty minutes.

Soon I was back at the tavern.

Ivan said, "You lasted twenty-nine minutes longer than most."

"Look at my hands."

"There's no way you can pour beer with those hands."

"Or hold a broom."

"I can't use you. Especially with how terrible a bartender you are. But you should have something to eat. At least, I owe you that much."

CHAPTER 35

MAGDEBURG

After a sandwich and a beer, I headed out of the tavern down the road toward the ship. Three miles later, I sat down. At this rate, I would be lucky to make it to the ship before it left without me. A minute later, what had been a clear day turned dark with storm clouds. I looked around and saw there was no shelter within miles. When it started to pour, I had no choice other than to sit and get soaked.

Just then, a horse and wagon stopped next to me. A beautiful woman sat in front, gripping the reins. She was fortunate enough to be holding an umbrella.

"What are you doing sitting in the rain?" she asked.

"Getting wet. I'm trying to get to America."

"You aren't going to get there sitting on the side of the road. Get on."

I got in the back, not daring to sit next to her.

"Don't be silly. Sit up here under this umbrella. I'm headed to Magdeburg. I can take you that far."

"What's in Magdeburg?"

"My husband. He went to pay his taxes in Hanover yesterday."

"Don't they come around to collect?"

"Yes, but they always seem higher that way. Some collectors ask for more money. That way, they get a little extra."

"Your husband is smart to do that."

"It's the only thing he's smart at. He's a terrible farmer. Do you know anything about farming?"

"Yes, I was a farmer in Bohemia."

"I heard Bohemians were good farmers."

"But not smart about paying taxes to the landlord, like your husband."

"If you need money, you can help on the farm for a while."

I needed to think about that. If I helped for a day or two, it would be some money. I could still make the ship.

The rain stopped just as we arrived at Magdeburg. She said, "There's my husband."

"He doesn't look too happy."

"The taxes must have been more than he thought."

"What are you doing sitting there with my wife? Get the hell out of here!"

I knew I should have ridden in the back. I had now lost my third job in one day.

CHAPTER 36

WE MEET AGAIN

We had stopped next to a tavern. I had enough money for one beer. Grandfather always said never to pass up a chance for a glass of beer.

I walked into the dimly lit tavern. I saw the Austrian, but he didn't see me. He was seated in the corner, talking to another man. Empty beer glasses sat in front of them. It looked like he was trying to trick the other man into getting drunk, just as he had done to me.

I had a couple of choices. I could go over and confront him and demand my money back, but he would deny everything. For all I knew, everyone might believe him and not believe me. The other thing I could do was wait for him to be alone and get my money back. After all, it was my money.

I would have to be very smart about this. I couldn't just walk up with other people around. He'd have to be alone. I went to the bar, keeping my back to him as much as possible. But he didn't seem to be paying any attention to me.

I ordered myself a beer with the last of my money. I decided to wait it out. I looked over at the Austrian. He seemed to be having a very good time with my money. That irritated me. If anybody was going to have a good time with my money, it should have been me. I hope he didn't spend it all. I needed that money to get to America.

I decided to check out the toilet. That's one time he might be alone. If he went in there, I could follow him in. Maybe, just maybe, I could surprise him and get my money back. I walked into the toilet. It looked and smelled like it hadn't been cleaned since the day it had been built. Even cows had a better place to shit and piss than the bar patrons had. I looked around and found a corner I could hide in. However, I didn't want to sit there until the Austrian went to the toilet.

I saw a window out the back that was big enough for a person to crawl through. I knew what I was going to do. I went out to the bar and sipped on my beer. An hour passed by. The Austrian just sat there. Didn't he ever have to go to the toilet? What kind of a man was he? I figured he was pretending to drink. That's probably what he had done to me. He hadn't had a sip to drink while I was downing the Slivovitz and beers.

I took another sip of my beer. It wasn't as good as Bohemian beer, but it was refreshing after spending my morning on the road. Then my chance came. The Austrian got up from his stool and ambled back to the toilet. I gave him about a minute and followed him.

As I was about to enter the toilet, another bar patron followed him in. So much for that idea. I certainly couldn't get my money back from him when someone else was in the toilet with us. I turned to walk back to the bar, waiting for another opportunity. Since the Austrian wasn't drinking that might not happen. The man entering the toilet turned around. Either he decided he didn't have to go or he didn't want to enter that foul-smelling room. He didn't go back to his table. He walked out the front door and probably chose to piss against the side of the tavern.

I turned and went into the toilet. The Austrian was standing against the wall, urinating, and I walked up behind him.

I said, "So there you are."

He didn't turn back. "Where else would I be to go to the toilet?"

"You don't remember me, do you?"

"Remember you. How can I? I can't even see you with my back to you."

"Certainly, you remember a Bohemian's voice who works hard for his money. That you ply with drinks and take his money when he's passed out."

He started to turn toward me, but his hands were occupied. I pushed him against the wall, with his back to me. I reached into his coat, where I had seen him keep his wallet. I grabbed the wallet and found his cash.

"What the hell do you think you're doing?"

I said, "I'm getting my money back."

"You can't do that."

"The hell I can't."

I looked in his wallet. He seemed to be pulling this trick on more people than just me. I debated whether I should take everything he had, but I decided otherwise. I just took what he had taken from me. Then I threw his wallet into the gutter where he had been pissing.

"What the hell! You didn't need to do that!"

"Yes, I did."

He got down on his knees, fishing for his wallet. I took that opportunity to jump out the open window in the back. I don't think he noticed me because he was so busy reaching for his wallet. I thought about going in to warn the man that the Austrian had been trying to cheat him, but I decided against that. My best course of action was to head out of town and head out of town quickly.

CHAPTER 37

NOT MY WIFE

I saw a man on a wagon headed on the road toward the ship. I ran toward it.

"Are you headed to Hamburg?"

"Not quite. About halfway there."

"Would you please give a poor Bohemian a ride? I'm trying to get to America."

He said, "I don't know why you'd want to do that. You'd be better off getting on a wagon and going in the other direction back home to Bohemia."

"No. I've decided to go to America."

"If there's no stopping you, hop on."

I scrambled in back, on top of sacks of wheat.

"Where are you going with all this?"

He said, "I'm off to sell my crops so I can pay the landlord."

"That's why I'm going to America. So I don't have to pay the landlord with all my hard-earned money."

"In America, you'll be lucky if you have money to pay yourself, from what I hear."

"What have you heard?" I asked.

"Things aren't as promising there as you may have heard."

"I heard there's free land available."

"That was then. This is now."

"What do you mean?" I asked.

"Years ago, they gave 120 acres free to people coming to settle their land and clear their woods. But that time is long gone now."

"You can't believe everything you hear."

He said, "I can believe this. My brother went there, and he wrote me a letter. He is heading back here as soon as he can scrape up enough cash to get on the next boat."

"I guess that's a German for you. Bohemians are tougher, I guess."

"Or not as smart," he said.

I didn't say what I wanted to say because I needed a ride. Instead, I said, "It doesn't matter. I don't need free land. I sent my brother money to buy some for me. I don't want to spend my life working for someone else. Working twelve hours a day. Barely making enough to have only bread, water, and potatoes for meals, except for meat on Sundays. A man can't live on that. My brother has raised enough crops for healthy meals and cows and pigs for sausages in America. That's what I want. Enough food for myself. That's all. Not to feed the landlords who have enough the way it is."

He said, "Do you have enough money to get to America?"

After remembering what happened to me with the Austrian, I decided not to tell him.

"No. I figure I'll just jump on the next ship."

As we rode along, I looked back to see if the Austrian was behind me. He probably figured, what could he do? He could report me to the police, but then

I could tell them it was my money. Not his. I laid down in between the sacks. Anyone following wouldn't see me. Why would they expect me to be hiding in there? They probably thought I might be hiding in one of the houses or another tavern or had returned the way I had come. Or I might have taken a back road. I had so many options they could consider; I wasn't too worried. That didn't keep me from looking.

"Why do you keep looking back?"

I decided not to tell the driver of the wagon the truth.

"My wife is following me."

She wasn't my wife yet, but my fiancé. It was the first time I had thought of her since I had left. I liked her better that way. She probably thought I was going to send for her when I got settled and it was time for her to join me in America. That time would never come.

"Shouldn't your wife be with you?"

"She's a witch."

"Most wives are," he said. "I'm fortunate. My wife isn't a witch. She is a good person. I'm blessed to have her."

"Maybe in America, I can find a woman like your wife, and I'd be lucky to have her as well."

"Good luck with that. From what I hear, there is a shortage of women in America. You might be living alone."

"Even that would be preferable. Living alone rather than living with the witch."

"You may think that now, but there is something about companionship. Even living with a witch might be preferable to living alone. Someone to talk to even if it is arguing."

I said, "I can do well enough arguing with myself."

"That's true. I argue with myself a lot, but that's one reason I picked you up this morning. I don't like arguing with myself."

"I don't mind it. At least one side of it is right."

"Also, you will need to find a hard-working woman."

"My wife, the witch, is the opposite of hard-working."

"That's unusual from what I hear. Bohemian women do all the work."

"My wife does a lot of work. But it's mostly getting me to do all the work. Even after I have done it."

"What did you do in Bohemia?" he asked.

"I was a farmer."

"So you know what it's like on a farm. How much work it's to get in a crop and hope it isn't destroyed by wind or hail. Or insects. In America, you might even have to face the Indians."

"I've heard about the Indians. Most are quite friendly, and where I'm going in Minnesota, some even come and share their food with the settlers and eat meals with them."

"Not the kind of Indians I've ever heard of. They are more likely to take scalps than a meal with you."

"It depends," I said. "If you were doing something mean to them, like taking their land, they would be mean to you. Where I'm going, it's mostly wooded. I'll clear the land and make money selling the lumber."

"That sounds easy. Too easy if you ask me."

"My brother has made a lot of money selling timber."

"Maybe so. Are you ready for the harsh winters in Minnesota?"

"I will build a cabin, stock up on food and firewood. I can tolerate the winter if I can do that."

"You'll be lucky if you can feed yourself. You'll wish for that bread, water, and potatoes that you had back in Bohemia."

"I don't believe that," I said.

"The next town up ahead is where I sell my crops. You'll have to get off there. I hope you make it to America. But more likely, I'll see you back here again someday. Probably heading back to your village in Bohemia."

"That will never happen."

"Never is a long time."

CHAPTER 38

MAN NEEDED

I still had a way to go to make it to my ship. I wanted to get there a day early to make sure the ship wouldn't leave without me. I didn't know if they did that, but I didn't want to take any chances. I stuck out my thumb.

A woman leaving town driving a buggy passed by without looking. Since she wasn't looking, she almost ran me over. Next came a man on a wagon. He looked to be in his forties, twice as old as me. He passed by me as well. Fine. I didn't want to ride with him anyway. But he stopped about fifty yards down the road. I didn't know if he was stopping for me or to rest the horses.

He yelled back, "You want a ride or not?"

"I'll take a ride."

I ran and jumped up onto the seat next to a well-dressed man with blonde hair and blue eyes.

"My name is Glen. Where are you headed?"

"I'm going to Hamburg for the ship to America."

"The Frisia, I think that's the name of it. That's the one that everyone takes," he said. "I don't know why you want to go there, though. There's plenty of opportunities here for a man like you."

"Not in Bohemia."

"But here there is. Matter of fact, I've got a farm. I'm looking for a man who might want to help me, and eventually, take over for me one of these days."

I said, "If you're looking at me, you're looking at the wrong man."

"Can you at least come to the farm and help unload this wagon full of feed?"

"I don't know. I want to make it to the ship on time."

"I'll even offer you a meal. My wife is a great cook."

"Okay, I could always use a good meal, and a guy's got to eat."

As we rode along, he told me he was among the wealthiest farmers. He owned more land than he could farm by himself. He hired people, but they soon left. He had to do more work than he could do in one day.

"And my daughter is no help. She would rather do housework."

We pulled up next to a house. It was a far nicer house than any I've seen back in Bohemia. We got off the wagon. A beautiful woman with blonde hair and blue eyes who must have been his daughter exited the house.

Helping on the farm and marrying his daughter might not be a bad proposition. I wouldn't have to clear any land or freeze in the winter. It all would have been done for me.

Then a blonde-haired, blue-eyed girl came out of the house. She was about eighteen and just as beautiful as the other woman who must have been her mother.

The mother came over and gave me a good hug. If she hugged me any closer, we'd probably have to get married.

After we unloaded the sacks, Glen invited me into the house. The supper was already set on the table.

Glen's wife, Glenda, welcomed me into the grand house. This family must be quite rich. The interior was spotless. These people didn't bring dirt from their chores back into the house after a day's work.

Glenda said, "We're just about to eat and have plenty of food."

Their daughter brought in bowls and platters of food.

"This is our daughter, Glenice."

Glenda sat me at the table. Glen took a place at one end of the table and Glenda at the other. Glenice sat beside me, sitting so close she was almost on top of me. It was some of the best food I've had in my whole life. I ate and ate until I couldn't eat anymore. Then I ate some more.

"I love a man who enjoys his food. So does my daughter, Glenice."

Glen said, "You must stay here tonight. You can't head out now. It's late, and you'll never catch a ride. Morning would be better."

After that meal, the idea of moving anywhere than to bed didn't interest me. So I accepted the offer. I went up to the bedroom and got on the bed. I hadn't ever slept on such a nice bed. I fell asleep instantly. When I woke up, it was pitch dark in the room. I did have to take a piss, but I was unsure where I would do this. I groped around in the dark and found a vase filled with flowers. Rather than stumble around in the night, I decided to piss in the vase. Probably not a very nice thing to do, but necessary. I put my head on the pillow. Then I heard the bedroom door creak open and slowly close.

I heard footsteps coming up to my bed. Soon, the covers were pulled back, and I felt a body next to mine. A warm, naked female body. She took one of my hands and put it on her breast.

"I hope you're not too tired," she said in a voice that sounded like Glenda.

"Wait! I can't do this."

"That's okay. I can."

She then moved down my body. This was a surprise. I didn't even think women did this sort of thing. I thought it was only a rumor that men just talked about and never really happened. It took everything in me to stop her.

"I can't do this. It isn't right."

"Who's to say what's right?"

"I guess I have to," I said.

I lifted her off me and off the bed.

"It's your loss."

"You may be right."

I heard her footsteps leave the bedroom. The door opened and closed. I don't know how long I rested there, congratulating myself for doing the right thing and kicking myself for passing up an offer I had to refuse. I was just about asleep when I heard the door open and close again. I again heard footsteps move to the side of the bed. Someone lifted the covers, and a naked body moved onto the bed beside me.

Was she back to try again? She was persistent, that's for sure. Then I realized the body was different; her breasts were smaller. It had to be the daughter. What was going on? Who were these people? Now the situation was different. It wasn't someone's wife offering herself to me, but a young woman who was available, willing, and, so far, very able. What she was doing to me, I had never experienced before. Things my fiancé in Bohemia had never done and had never thought of doing.

Then something happened. Or didn't happen. Even though my mind was willing to enjoy this young girl, my body had different ideas.

"This isn't working," I said.

"That's for sure. What's wrong?"

"It isn't you. It's me."

"That's for sure."

She slid off the bed and tip-toed out of the bedroom.

I closed my eyes, and when I opened them, it was daylight already. I smelled bacon frying downstairs. I heard chatter and pots and pans clanging. I decided to get up. Then I saw the vase and noticed that the flowers were already wilting. What was I going to do with those flowers?

I opened the window and tossed them out. I got dressed and walked down to the kitchen. Glen was sitting at the table, ready for his breakfast. I sat down in the same spot I had taken the night before.

"Would you like some breakfast and coffee?" Glenda asked.

She didn't wait for an answer but came over, set a heaping breakfast in front of me, and poured me a cup of coffee. When Glen looked away, Glenda reached down between my legs. I jerked away from her and bumped the table when I stood up.

"What's going on," Glen asked.

"I wasn't paying attention and spilled the coffee," she said as she wiped the non-existent coffee off my lap.

Then Glenice came in and sat down next to me.

Glen asked, "Did you decide to stay with us and help us farm? And marry my daughter, Glenice, here?"

"No, I'm on my way to the ship today, and I have to get there before it leaves."

"You're still going?" Glen asked.

"No, you can't go," Glenice said.

"I thought you were going to do your best to make him stay, Glenice."

"I tried everything to make him stay. Well, almost everything."

Glenda took the full plate out from in front of me. The coffee too. Glen handed my coat and bag to me. I must have outstayed my welcome.

CHAPTER 39

PULLING AN AUSTRIAN

I ended up having to walk about halfway to the ship. I did catch a few rides, but they were very uncomfortable. On one, I was packed in with a bunch of pigs in the back of a wagon. By the time I got off, I looked and smelled more like a pig than a person.

On the next ride, a woman asked me to sit up front with her. When she smelled the pigs, she kicked me off her wagon. That ride lasted about ten yards.

A day later, I arrived at the port and found the dock. A mean-looking man sat at a desk, registering people for passage on the ship. A line that stretched for more than a block moved slower than my brother Josef who took all day when he was asked to do the easiest of chores.

It was a hot day, and the sun beat down upon me. I thought I would never get to the table to sign in. When I got to the table, the mean-looking man closed his book. I handed my papers to him. He looked at me, looked at my papers, and looked at me.

He said, "I can't let you on the ship."

"Why not? Have my papers expired?"

"Your papers are fine, but the person in front of you was the last person allowed on the ship."

"Can't you let me on anyway?"

"No, we have regulations," he said. "Only so many people are allowed on the ship."

"I'm just a small person. I don't take up much space. You can hang me off the side if you want."

"No, rules are rules. You would put us over the limit. I don't want to lose my shipping contract."

"You mean, that's it? I missed it by one person?"

"Yes."

I said, "If I hadn't stunk like a pig, I would have made it."

"I don't know what that means. Even so, I cannot let you on board."

"If someone doesn't get on board, can I take his place?"

"I can put you on a list. You would be the next person if someone doesn't show up. Or you can wait for another ship."

After he took my name, I walked over to the tavern. When I walked in, I saw plenty of men with bags and suitcases at the bar. I didn't want to wait for another ship, so I asked if anybody was going on the Frisia. Almost everyone raised his hand.

"I will pay someone to give up their spot. They can take the next ship out."

There were no takers.

"Why don't you take the next ship out?"

"My passport expires today. If I don't get out today, I have to go back to Bohemia."

"Then go back to Bohemia!"

"I must get to America. People are waiting for me."

"People are waiting for us too."

So I had no takers. I saw someone sitting in a corner drinking a beer. I thought if it worked for the Austrian, it might work for me. I sat down with him.

I said, "Are you going out on the ship?"

"Yes. As soon as they board, I'm out of here."

"You have papers?"

"Oh yes, I have papers. They are good for another month or so. But I wanted to get to America as soon as possible."

I asked, "How about if I buy you a beer and Slivovitz for your journey?"

"That's very kind of you."

Soon, one drink led to many others. By the ninth drink, he was face down on the table. I had pulled the Austrian's trick and had only had one beer. I had to have one. After all, I was in a bar.

Someone came in and said, "Anyone boarding the Frisia, the ship is boarding now. Please meet at the gangplank."

Whatever a gangplank was.

Everyone headed out, so I did too. When I got there, I watched as one passenger after another boarded the ship. I stood to the side of the mean-looking man who was letting people on. The man I treated to beers and Slivovitz was nowhere in sight. Soon the man at the table announced that it was the last call. I went up to him.

"Is there room?"

"Yes. One person hasn't shown up. If he's not here in one minute, I will let you on board."

I looked into the crowd, waiting and hoping my drinking partner wouldn't appear. Off in the distance, just as a minute was about to expire, I saw him leave the tavern.

"Check me in," I said.

He took my name, looked at my papers, and said, "Get on board. You're going to America."

CHAPTER 40

THE LAST THING I NEEDED

As I walked up the gangplank, I looked back at my drinking partner. He was almost to the table to sign in. I didn't hear what he had to say, but I saw his hands raise in anger and his fists go up. When I got on deck, he looked up and saw me. His fists rose even higher. He spoke some swear words in German, which I knew. I yelled swear words back to him in Bohemian. Then I ducked into a corner to hide so I wouldn't be kicked off the ship.

I've never seen so many people in one place in my whole life. With this many people, I hoped that America had enough room for all of us. There were mothers with crying babies. There were older men, barely able to move, who I didn't think would ever last the journey to America. I wondered if I would. They told me there was one bathroom for every hundred people. I thought I needed one for myself. Did they have enough provisions on the ship for everyone on board? I didn't see how that was possible.

There were so many people I could barely walk along the ship's deck without stopping every few inches. A woman yelled at me for stepping on her little boy's foot.

"I didn't do it on purpose. I'm sorry."

"Sorry doesn't help. What good will my boy be with a bad foot in America?"

I wandered down some stairs to another level. There were even more people down there if that was possible. I heard music. Someone was playing an accordion. A Bohemian was playing a song for the journey to America. I recognized the song.

I walked up to him. I knew the words and tried singing, although not very well. A smile came to his face, and he started singing along. Soon, a few others joined in. Within minutes, everyone in the lower deck was singing the song.

To translate, it was the "Marianka" waltz. It was about a man walking along who sees a woman. He says, 'Come lay with me. Come lay with me in my bed so nice.'

There's a dirtier version, but I didn't think the crowd would want to sing that verse.

Then he played the "Green Meadow" waltz. I wondered if there would be green meadows in Minnesota. I was told it would only be woods. But soon, I would clear the land of trees and make a green meadow on my property.

When that song was over, someone who had smuggled some beer on board poured a glass for me. The beer went down like all good beer, smooth and quick. I was feeling pretty good and happy to be on my way.

The ship pulled away from the dock. I could feel the boat swaying back and forth. If this was as bad as it gets, it wouldn't be a problem. I didn't even have trouble standing up.

I heard the ship whistle. The man I tricked didn't make it on board. But he could get on a later ship, where I couldn't have. I would have lost my chance to leave for a new country. I hope he didn't catch up to meet the ship somewhere else. The last thing I needed was an enemy in a foreign land. However, I didn't feel too bad because he drank many drinks I paid for.

The ship seemed to be moving faster and rocked back and forth even more. Now, this was getting serious, I thought. I would be okay if this was as bad as it got.

I turned and saw a woman standing next to me. She was about my age, had long, black hair, and a mouth a little too large for her face. She wore a black dress that stopped just below her knees. She smiled up at me.

I said in Bohemian, "Do I know you?"

She answered in Bohemian, "No, you don't. Are you excited about going on the voyage?"

"The voyage, not so much. I'm looking forward to the new land and starting a new life. How about you?"

"Yes. I've waited for this day for many years."

She looked up at me and smiled again. It was a beautiful smile. My fiancé never smiled like that. Mostly she just laughed at me and told me how ridiculous I was. Yes, I was. At one time, I had intended to marry her. Not now. The woman next to me was the last thing I needed. I didn't need to be stuck with a woman before getting to Minnesota. I had a goal. I wanted to clear the land of trees and build a cabin with the logs from those trees. Then get a cow and a pig and plant some crops. Maybe then I could think of a woman. That was somewhere down the road.

I moved away from the young woman. Every time I turned, I saw her beside me. My older brother had the same problem with dogs. They would follow him around just as this woman followed me.

I ducked into the toilet. I spent as much time there as possible before someone knocked on the door. When I got out, she was standing there waiting. This was going to be a problem. One that I had to figure out.

I decided to make myself as disgusting as possible. I spat out a chew of tobacco on the floor next to her. She wouldn't want someone as messy as that for a partner. Someone who spits on the floor. She didn't budge. Instead, she spat a chew of tobacco next to mine.

I hoped that didn't mean we were married.

CHAPTER 41

A POUND OF BEER

I had been on board the Frisia for several days. It was hard for me to determine how many days since I was down below, and I couldn't tell day from night. A storm had passed through at one point, rocking the ship back and forth and tilting it off to the side. I was sure I would have slid off and into the Atlantic Ocean if I had been on deck.

My stomach didn't agree with the motion of the ship and rebelled forcefully. The toilet was unavailable. The rebellion landed upon a couple of my fellow travelers with no good response from them. I couldn't be singled out since I wasn't the only one.

Later I started to feel a little better because the ocean wasn't rebelling either. I felt the ship slow and come to a stop. This trip wasn't so bad. I don't know what everyone was complaining about. The time for the voyage across the Atlantic had passed very quickly.

Someone came down and told us we had to leave the ship. He didn't have to tell me twice. I was anxious to see my new land. When we got to the upper deck, many people were walking down the gangplank, but without their belongings. If they had any bags, they had left them behind. I had my bag with me.

When I got to the bottom of the gangplank, a man took my name and said, "You are free to roam around for the day. Be back tomorrow at 8:00 in the morning."

"Eight in the morning! Why would I do that? We are in New York. Why do I have to be back on the ship?"

"New York, hell. We are in England, restocking the ship for a voyage to America. The trip here was just a drop in the ocean."

"If this was a drop, I hate to see the whole ocean."

"Be back by eight o'clock. Or the ship will leave without you."

"Can I wait on board?" I asked him because I didn't want to be left behind.

"No, everyone must vacate the ship so it can be cleaned. As you surely notice, it needs a thorough cleaning after what occurred during the last few days."

"Yeah, you got that right. What am I to do?"

"A tavern is kept open all night for those who wish. Or else you may wait at the harbor station. They have benches. Of the two, the tavern would be my preference."

I walked into the tavern and sat with my back to the wall facing the entrance. It was a good thing I did that. No sooner had I sat down when I saw the man I had cheated entering. How did he get here so fast? There must have been another ship. Only after he got closer did I realize it wasn't the same man, but someone who looked like him.

Even though I had decided not to drink, I did have a beer. That wouldn't cause me any problems. I also ordered a sandwich. The bartender asked me for the money in pounds. I didn't know how much my money weighed. I held out some coins. The bartender took all my money and didn't give any back to me. I thought maybe I shouldn't have held out so many coins if he was going to take whatever I offered. The sandwich arrived, but it wasn't enough to feed a bird.

The night passed slowly. People wandered in and out. Others fell asleep at the table. Bartenders woke them up and told them that unless they were awake and drinking, they would have to leave.

That was the slowest I had ever consumed a beer in my life. Soon, the darkness outside changed to light. I looked up at the clock and saw that it was six o'clock. I didn't want to miss the ship. I decided to wait by the dock until we could board the Frisia.

When I got there, the man at the table said. "You got here just in time. We are just ready to lift the gangplank."

"What? It's only six o'clock. The ship isn't due to leave until eight."

"I don't know where you got six o'clock. It's eight o'clock on my watch, and that's what we go by."

I figured the clock at the bar had to be wrong, either by accident or intentionally. I was glad I decided to be early, or I would have missed the ship and missed my chance for America.

CHAPTER 42

SHE COULD EAT

I got back on board and went down to the lower deck. It seemed as if everyone had taken the same seats as before. It was as if the seats had been assigned to them. My spot next to the toilet was vacant, which I thought was a wise choice considering I might be visiting there quite often.

"How long is this voyage?" I asked.

"Longer than you would want. Some say three weeks. Some say seven days."

"Why the difference?"

"I guess it depends on the weather and the currents. Or if the captain gets lost and takes you to Spain instead of America."

He must have been joking. I don't think any captain would mistake America for Spain, but you never know. No sooner had I settled in my spot, when I looked over to my left. My woman friend from earlier sat down next to me.

"It looks like you're going to need company on this trip."

That was the last thing I needed, but I kept quiet. She snuggled up closer to me even though there was enough space next to her. I moved over a bit and faced away from her towards the toilet, preferring that to her. She just sidled up closer to me. Yes, this was going to be a long journey to America. If I had a choice of a person to sit next to me on this trip, she would be the last person. It turns out she was the last person.

Soon, the ship pulled away from the dock and gradually sped up until what I imagined was full speed. We were on the Atlantic Ocean, headed to our destination.

"My name is Jana."

"Jana. Where are you headed to in the new world?"

"I'm headed to New York, just like you are."

I meant after that, but I didn't ask her any more questions, fearing she might talk to me. She talked to me anyway.

"I come from Czechoslovakia, north of Prague."

I said, "Northern Czech is an entirely different land from where I came from."

"I know. Some of your words are strange."

I thought all of her words were even stranger to me. I wish she had been a stranger. She decided that she wanted to talk. And talk she did. She spoke for hours and hours on end about anything and everything I didn't want to hear about. So I remained silent.

She said, "My name is Jana."

"Yes, you told me that."

"And back home, I've been told I eat a lot. That I eat from when the sun comes up until the sun comes up again."

I looked at her and said, "My goodness. You don't look like you eat that much. You're skinny and scrawny."

I think she took this as a compliment which was the opposite of how I had intended it.

"People ask me how come I don't get fat. I tell them I burn up all this food by talking all the time."

If that were true, no food would be left in her home village, which is probably why they sent her to America.

She talked more and more about herself. Her father. Her two brothers. Her sisters. She had six sisters, and I would rather have had any of her sisters next to me. Or even either of her two brothers, for that matter.

I thought maybe if I got up and moved, I'd get away from her. That didn't work, because after I had used the toilet, I moved across the way and sat down, and she sat next to me. The space was smaller than she could manage to fit into but fit she did. We were even closer together now than we had been before.

CHAPTER 43
SILENT

It seemed like we had been on the ship for years. If the voyage lasted fifteen days, I was sure she would run out of words to say.

I was proven wrong. She had more words than there were insects in the world. That's a lot of words because everywhere you look, there are insects.

She told me of the time she went to bring in the cows from the field. It had started raining. It rained so hard with lightning and thunder she took shelter in an old shack. Lightning struck the shed and set it on fire.

"So you had to move?" I asked.

"No, it was raining so hard, it put the fire out. I didn't have to move because lightning doesn't strike in the same place twice. I was perfectly safe there."

Obviously, she had been safe because here she was sitting next to me.

"When I finally got the cows back into the barn, my father asked what took me so long. I told him I was almost killed by lightning. He told me that would have been better than getting the cows in late for milking. I knew right then and there that my father didn't think much of me."

"What was your first clue?"

She laughed. She had a pretty laugh and a pretty smile too. If only she didn't talk so damn much.

Then she said, "You don't say much, do you?"

I thought, if I did have something to say, I wouldn't be able to get more than two or three words out fast enough without her starting in on the next sentence. She had a point there. People in my village called me Tichy, meaning silent. Some thought it was a strange nickname. I thought it was perfect. I had heard that silence is golden.

And I'd rather be golden than skinny like Jana.

CHAPTER 44

DEAD IN THE WATER

It seemed like I had been on the ship for an entire lifetime. I had made a mark on the side of the wall each day I had been on board. I couldn't determine the number of days by that because I couldn't tell whether it was day or night. I marked it by periods of sleep, and it seemed like I was sleeping all the time. For all I knew, I might have been on the ship for only one day.

I asked my fellow travelers when they thought we would get there. They had no idea. They told me we'd get there when we get there. Well, I knew that.

Every once in a while, a crew member would come down and check on us. I don't know what they'd do if they found any problems. The only time they did anything was when someone died. They would carry that person above deck. I wondered what they did with them after that.

If people were sick, they kept them separated from those who were healthy. It seemed like half the lower deck was filled with sick people, and the other half with people waiting to get sick. I was lucky. I had gotten my sickness out of the way earlier.

I still had my companion with me. My unwanted companion as far as I was concerned. She was glued to my side. No matter what I tried to do, she was there.

The only time I was free of her was when I went to the toilet. It wouldn't surprise me at all if she followed me in there. I even went in many times when I didn't have to use the toilet, only to get away from her.

She continued her non-stop talking. Even when I was asleep, she talked to me because I'd wake up, and she would be muttering one thing or another. She'd ask me questions that I didn't know the answer to. Even if I did, I didn't have a chance to answer her.

You would think someone talking that much might have something interesting to say. None of it was interesting. It was like listening to the constant drone of the engines, which I would have preferred. She went on just as they did, non-stop all day.

Then the engines stopped. I don't know how far we were. Had we arrived in America? I surely hoped so. I heard yelling above. They weren't cries of joy but sounds of trouble. I had heard that sound many times in my life.

A few people ventured above deck even though they weren't allowed. A few minutes later, one of them returned and announced to all that we were dead in the water. Yes, maybe we were. If the engines were dead, we might be too.

He said, "The engines have stopped running."

I already knew that. There was a breakdown of some kind and we were going nowhere. I thought if the ship had sails, we could at least go somewhere with the wind's power. The Frisia wasn't equipped for that. I heard of ships that traveled with sails that stalled in the water due to the lack of wind. They should have had ships that used both. Maybe they do, but this ship wasn't one of them.

"Do they know how long it'll take to fix?"

"As long as it takes," the man said.

There was that answer again. There was never a definite answer for anything. Just as long as it takes. Each minute the ship wasn't moving was another minute I would be subjected to the words of the woman who stuck next to me. If only she would stick to some other man on the ship, my problem would be his. I was anxious to get to Minnesota, but I was even more anxious with her next to me.

"Did they say what part is broken?"

"The camshaft," someone said as fact.

"No, a piston rod," another said.

"Some people said it was the propeller shaft."

I didn't know what a propeller shaft was, but it sounded serious. If something that propelled the boat wasn't working, it was a big problem. How do you get parts to fix something like that in the middle of the ocean? Did they carry replacements on board? If they did, they'd have to bring one of everything in case something broke down, and I didn't think they did that. They just assumed that nothing would break down, which is like a farmer hoping that no disease, pests, or drought would damage his crops.

Things happen, and you have to make them unhappen.

"What are they going to do?" I asked.

"They have someone aboard who might be able to fix it, but he is an apprentice. The main repairman didn't make this voyage," a crew member answered.

Of course, he didn't. Why would he? What could a trainee apprentice do to help fix the problem? He probably had no more idea how to fix the propeller shaft than the woman next to me. She probably had a better idea. I was resigned to spending the rest of my days on that ocean and never making it to America.

Did they have enough rations on the Frisia? They only had food for a certain number of days, and if the ship wasn't moving, we might run out of food. The thought of starving to death on the ocean didn't appeal to me. Of course, starving to death anywhere didn't appeal to me either.

And what about this poor girl next to me? As much as she ate, she would wither to nothingness. I guess I could always hope for that.

I tried to sleep. She kept nudging me awake and talking about an old goat. It was a very dull story. She told me what the goat ate. It was the same thing every day. It turns out the family sold it from under her, and she would miss it. Maybe the goat left of its own accord, so it wouldn't have to listen to her.

As I tried to sleep, I heard the sound of clanging metal resounding throughout the ship. They were hard at work repairing whatever needed to be fixed. I waited for the sound to stop, hoping we would soon be on our way.

I wondered if I could do something to help. I was good at machinery. I had done some repairs on the farm. I snuck out of the hold and went to the source of the racket. Whatever they were doing required a lot of noise.

When I reached the engine compartment, I saw three men. One was pounding, and the other two were hard at work watching. Parts were strewn about the floor. From the looks of it, the apprentice had dismantled everything and had no idea how to reassemble it. Looking at it, I could see how it fit together, even though I didn't know what it was. I've always been able to do this with machinery. Something about the way my mind worked.

I walked up to them and asked if I could help them. One of them understood me and told me I could help by returning to where I belonged.

"I belong in America, and you're not helping me get there. I'm good at this. Let me help."

They were insistent. However, I was even more insistent. I grabbed the hammer out of the man's hand. I looked at what he was doing. Where he had learned his trade, I'll never know. We would be on the ocean forever if we left *it up to him. He mentioned something about going to the captain. I wished he would because I would tell him what I thought of his apprentice mechanic.*

When I examined what he was trying to do, I knew it would never work. The original part had broken in half. I've seen it on the farm many times. There had been too much stress on it. The captain may have been trying to overwork the engine just as my father on the farm would do. I knew no matter how much the apprentice pounded, he wouldn't get this part in place. He was putting everything in incorrectly. It was like putting square pegs in round holes.

"You are doing this the wrong way," I said.

"It's the right way. It's the only way it'll fit."

"An idiot could do a better job of this."

"And I suppose you're just the idiot."

"No, that would be you."

The assistant brought the captain over, who immediately started swearing at me in Norwegian or another language I didn't understand. I knew swearing when I heard it. I just ignored him and went on with my work. I was sure I would be arrested for failing to follow orders, but I would be alive and arrested. The jail on the ship would be better than the woman that stuck to me like glue.

After I finished replacing the part, I stood back. The apprentice grabbed the wrench from me to finish the job. I stopped him before he caused more damage than he had already done.

I said, "Didn't you see what you were doing? You were doing it incorrectly. You put this part on backward. That would never work unless you wanted to go backward to where we came from."

The captain looked at me and the apprentice. They nodded to each other. The captain barked some orders. When the engines roared to life, the ship moved ever so slightly. It looked like this was going to work. At least it was getting us somewhere, and somewhere was better than nowhere.

The captain came over to me and said some words to me. A crewman translated for me.

"The captain wants to know if you would like to work on the ship."

"I'm not under arrest?"

"No, the captain is pleased with your work."

"Then I accept. Gladly."

I would do anything to get away from that woman on the lower deck.

Soon, I was up in the crew's quarters eating a fine meal. The crewman pointed to a bunk where I could sleep.

"You will be needed later. There are many things to repair on the ship, and if the captain is going to pay you, he wants work out of you."

Pay me?! That was even better. I was willing to do this for nothing, but I was going to be paid. I asked the crewman how many days before we got to New York. He told me it would be about five days. Five days in these quarters were much better than five days down in the lower deck.

I laid down in the bunk and fell right asleep. It was hot in there, but it was quiet. It was the first peace I had gotten on board the ship. I was awakened by the interpreter.

"You have to leave," he said.

I knew it was too good to be true.

"Your wife was wondering where you were."

"My wife? I don't have a wife."

"She says you do. She insists we can't have you separated. She can be very insistent. There is a spare crew's quarters that is empty. You two can take that room."

"Do I have to?" I asked.

"Yes. She is a member of the crew as well. She will help cook the meals."

With her in the kitchen near all that food, we might run out of food before tomorrow.

CHAPTER 45

A PIECE OF MY MIND

The last five days on the ship were like a vacation. There weren't very many repairs to make. I fixed some things even a child could repair, but the apprentice couldn't. I was waiting for my repair to fail. However, it held up for the entire five days. The captain seemed very grateful to me and offered me a bonus and a permanent job on his ship for the voyage back to England. England wasn't where I wanted to go. I had been to England and hadn't cared much for it. I was anxious to get to Minnesota and my land.

Jana enjoyed her time on the ship, especially in the kitchen. She'd eat about three meals for each one she prepared. The other cooks on board didn't understand her. They just shook their heads at her constant chattering.

Each day, I would wander into the kitchen and ask Jana, when I got a word in edgewise, to prepare food to take below. Then I would sneak it below deck to the hungry people. If questioned, I would say it was for the mechanic or the first mate, and the captain had ordered me. Soon they no longer asked me.

When I got below, a crowd would surround me and almost tackle me. After that, I worried about my safety and set it down at the bottom of the steps and moved quickly to the main deck. I would have done the same thing as them if I had been down there. When one is hungry, a man will do almost anything. I had been starved and thirsty down there and preferred having a healthy meal every day.

Another positive about being a crew member was that I was now allowed on the main deck. Until that time, I hadn't seen the ocean. I hadn't imagined it to be as huge as it was. It seemed to go on forever in every direction. The first people to sail across must have been very courageous.

One day, I looked over the side and spotted a large fish swimming alongside the ship. I asked a fellow crewman what it was. He told me it wasn't a fish but a whale. It looked like it could destroy the ship with its tail. As the whale swam out, a spout of water shot out of its back as if saying goodbye and good riddance to us. Before ships, these whales had the whole ocean to themselves. Now they had to share it with people. I bet they didn't like it the day that happened. I wonder if people would appreciate it if these whales marched on to land, and we'd have to share the land with them. I don't think that would last too long.

I didn't realize how much I had missed seeing the sun rise and set each day and seeing the stars come out at night and the moon as it made its journey across the sky. In Minnesota, I would watch the sun come up every day and watch it set each night on property that belonged to me. That's something that wasn't possible in Bohemia where only the wealthy landlords were entitled to land.

I kept looking over the horizon to see if I could see America. Instead, all I saw every day was more water.

On the main deck, I saw very wealthy people wearing fine clothes. They lounged on chairs and had people waiting on them. Whatever the crew did wasn't enough. After all, they were getting paid, so they were expected to put up with crap from the rich.

I thought of the people down below who had nothing. They had barely a spot to lay their head at night. The people below seemed happier. Whenever I went to the lower deck, I heard an accordion playing and people singing. Some even got up and danced if they had room. I wondered how so much happiness and joy could come from people with nothing.

On the main deck, the wealthy people complained about this or that or the other thing. How come dinner was late? How come it's going to rain? It will ruin my day. I'm so bored. There is nothing to do. They had so many complaints. I just wanted to go there and give them a piece of my mind. It would do no good, and I probably would get sent down to the lower deck.

I would play little tricks on them. When they weren't looking, I would take some item of theirs and put it with another person. A big fight would start when the first person discovered it missing and a fellow traveler had it. Why would I take something like that, they would say. I have more of those than I could ever use. That was the way of the world. The wealthy had more of anything than they could ever use. It was never enough. Then they took even more from hard-working people.

The captain would have to settle the argument. I stood off to the side and laughed. It brought me great joy to entertain these wealthy people because they seemed to take great pleasure in the disagreement.

They were used to arguing over property.

CHAPTER 46

LIKE GLUE

Next to me was the woman of glue, Jana. Would I ever be rid of her? We slept in the same bed each night, but even though we were in the same bed, I was alone. Nothing happened between us. I was content with keeping it that way. Each night, she tried to make advances toward me. With each advance, I moved away from her. Soon she had the bed to herself, and I slept on the floor, which made it a more peaceful night's sleep for me.

One night, she asked, "Don't you like me?"

"It isn't a matter of like or not like."

"What is it then?"

"It's a matter of me wanting to be alone or not alone. And I would like to be alone."

"How can anyone want to be alone?"

"If I'm alone, I never make mistakes. Because if I do, I'm the only one who knows about it. I'm not constantly reminded every day of my mistakes. I had a fiancé back in Bohemia who did a wonderful job of that. Soon, I thought less of myself than she thought of me. Which was something I didn't think was possible."

Jana said, "I would never do that. Have I ever said an unkind word to you?"

"With all you've said, I've stopped paying attention. You go on and on and on, and eventually, your words scramble together, and I don't remember anything you are talking about. Except for something about a goat."

"See, you do listen to me."

"Yes, but I will be like that goat. I will be gone from you when we reach land."

I looked, and there was sadness in her eyes.

"You mean you don't want me to be with you in New York?"

"I don't want to be with you anywhere. Not even on this ship."

She looked even more hurt.

Finally, she said, "I don't care what you say. When we get to New York, we'll be married."

One day, I heard someone shout from the top of the ship, "Land Ho!"

I didn't know what Ho was, but I figured Ho was the name of a country or an island we would pass before America. I soon learned that we were about to enter New York. This part of my journey would be over. It would be nice to get on solid ground again. I looked at the city moving toward us.

We watched as the ship pulled up to the dock. I don't know how the captain could have guided a ship this huge into such a small area. People lined up along the pier, looking at the Frisia like they had never seen a ship before. Perhaps, they never had. They waved at us, and we waved at them. It seemed like they were welcoming us to their land. Then I saw people making other gestures which made me think the opposite. There had to be some who wanted this country for themselves and themselves only.

The gangplank was lowered, and passengers filed off the ship. Passengers were led to the Customs House at Castle Gardens for processing. The first to be processed, of course, were the very wealthy who had people carrying their bags for them. When they got ashore, they were greeted by other men who took their bags and stowed them on carriages and buggies. It was as if they had just taken a Sunday ride in the country. It would be a lot different for the people below. For me too. We would have to go through this place called Immigration. I was told by a crewman that if I liked lines, I would like Immigration. I hated lines. If I never saw another line in my life, I would be quite happy.

A man checked everybody's papers. Then he rechecked them to make sure we were allowed to come into their country.

Finally, it was my turn. I got to the man, and he looked at my papers and said, "Vojta Sitec. I see from your papers that you are allowed to come into this country. Are you alone?"

I was about to say yes when Jana said, "I'm his wife."

Before I could say no, the man asked for her papers.

Jana said, "I have my old papers with my old name on them. We were married on the ship. The captain married us. So I'm his wife".

I started to protest, but before I could get a word out, the man said it was okay for us to enter. Jana dragged me away.

I said, "What do you think you're doing? You are not my wife."

"As far as America is concerned, I'm your wife."

I was never going to be rid of this woman. She would be next to me no matter what I tried to do.

She said, "Now that we're here, we can settle in New York."

"I don't know what you're talking about."

"You are a good mechanic. I'm sure they need good mechanics in New York. You can get a good job. We can get a good home. You can take care of me, and we can have as many children as you'd like."

"I don't need anyone to take care of me. I already have as many children as I want. Which is none."

"It's only right for every married couple to have as many children as they want."

"We're not married! You can have as many children as you want, but you'll have to do it without my help. I'm not taking part in any of this. I came to America to be free."

She said, *"I came to America to live in New York."*

"There are too many people here. I want to go to Minnesota."

"What is this place, Minnesota? I have never heard of it. How come you are just telling me about this now?"

"You can get your place here in New York, but I will be headed west on the next steamboat out of New York."

"There are Indians out west."

"They won't bother me."

"It would bother me. They would certainly take advantage of a woman like me. I wouldn't be safe out there."

"They wouldn't be safe with you out there."

"My brother told me where to catch the first boat. That's where I'm going."

"Wait. I'm going with you."

"I thought you didn't want any part of going to Minnesota."

"It might not be so bad if I'm with you."

"It might be so bad if I'm with you," I said.

"Oh, always joking around, aren't you? You'll need someone to cook for you. I'm a good cook, and I will take care of you."

"I don't need anyone to take care of me. I'll end up taking care of you, is more likely."

How was I going to get rid of her? If she wanted to go to Minnesota, how was I going to stop her? I looked around to see if any other eligible young men were alone to take Jana. I knew as soon as they spent a few minutes with her, they would want to be rid of her too.

We walked along the busy streets of New York. We badly needed a bath, so the sidewalks weren't so crowded for us. We did get lost, but eventually, we found the steamboat ticket office. I paid for my trip.

She said, "What about me? I have no money."

It looked like I would have to pay for her way as well as mine. Maybe at one of the stops, she would decide that she had had enough and let me continue without her.

"I only have money for myself to get to Minnesota."

"It's not right. A man should pay for his wife's way."

"You are not my wife!" I said.

"Ask the man back there. He'll tell you I am."

CHAPTER 47

NO REWARD

We were on a steamboat traveling from New York to Albany on the Hudson River. Just outside of Catskill, the steamboat captain misjudged a turn. The steamboat ran aground. As much as he tried paddling the rear wheel back and forth and back and forth, the boat wouldn't budge. He ordered all passengers off to lighten the load.

I marched off the steamboat with Jana close behind. We joined a group of passengers sitting under an old oak tree. Some fancy-dressed people were complaining about the inconvenience. The rest of us took it in stride. I knew things never went as planned, so when something went wrong, it seemed like it was part of the plan. I'd had enough boats for a while, so I didn't mind the time on land. This town looked nice. I was almost tempted to stay here. Jana must have read my thoughts.

"Why don't we just stay here?"

"That's an option. You're free to stay if you want, but I'm heading on."

"Then, so am I."

The steamboat captain came ashore and gathered all the able-bodied men.

"If you would please get into the water at the front of the boat. At my signal, you can assist by pushing the boat back off the sandbar."

Nothing about this trip from Bohemia had been easy. Why start now? I waded into the water, followed closely behind by Jana. She wasn't going to let me out of her sight for one second. We pushed and pushed and couldn't move that steamboat even an inch. The captain had done a good job of it.

We all got back on shore, and the captain announced, "We are stranded here until another boat comes along to help."

I had no interest in waiting. An idea came to me. I approached the captain and said, "How about if a few men went to nearby farms? They could ask for teams of horses to help free the steamboat."

The person Jana and I talked to was a farmer by the name of John Swenson. He didn't seem too eager to use his horses for this purpose.

I said, "The captain will pay you nicely."

"How much?"

"He didn't say, but he told me you would be rewarded."

I guess that was enough to make him come along. When we arrived at the riverbank, we were met by a dozen teams of horses. Most looked like they could barely pull their weight. Others were Arabians and other mighty steeds. I figured if they couldn't move this boat, with the help of us pushing, nothing could move it.

We tried and couldn't move the steamboat. We heard the sound of a steam whistle from the other side of a hill. Then a giant steam tractor appeared with its iron lugs digging into the soil. Soon the horses and tractor were hooked to the steamboat. The men took their positions, ready to push. Some of the horses stood knee-deep in the water. I hoped no people or horses drowned or the captain would pay mightily, and I would probably be blamed.

We heard the sound of 'heave-ho.' Then all the horses flexed their muscles, and the ropes tensed. The big wheel in the back turned. It seemed like it had moved. First, an inch. Then two inches. Then a foot. Soon, the boat drifted off the sandbar. A few men tripped and fell into the water, but I just hung on to the boat.

The horses were untied. The ones in the water were led ashore. Swenson walked up to the captain. I knew what he was going to ask, so I listened.

"What do you mean, no reward?"

The captain said, "I didn't promise any reward. Anyone who told you that is a liar."

Swenson came looking for me. If he found me, I would stay in this town forever, never to leave again. I would have a permanent place in the town's graveyard.

One thing I did know how to do, and that was hide. I borrowed a woman's hat and shawl, put them on, and stood in the middle of a group of women. Swenson would have to search through all the women to get to me, and he had no interest in doing that. I knew I wouldn't want to confront these women myself. They weren't a group to be messed with. Soon, Swenson and the other farmers gave up and returned to their farms. I got out of my disguise and got onto the boat. Of course, Jana was next to me. I couldn't hide from her.

After we got on board, I heard the captain praising himself for his great idea when it had been my idea all along. I was ready to tell him that, but he might kick me off the boat, and I didn't want that to happen.

Jana looked at me and said, "That was pretty smart of you."

"You would think he would have given me a reward of some kind."

"Your reward is me, I guess."

How did I get to be so lucky?

CHAPTER 48

A LOT TO LEARN

The steamboat stopped in a city in New York called Albany. It wasn't as large as New York City but larger than any in Bohemia.

"Now what?" Jana asked.

"Next we have to get on a train to Buffalo."

"I've never been on a train before. I wonder what that's like."

"I suppose just like a ship, except you can't drown," I said.

I asked someone for directions to the railway station.

He said, "Just follow this street down here, go two blocks, take a right at the auditorium, go one block, go left, and walk four blocks until you see a sign that says Grand Central Station. You can't miss it."

"I hate it when someone tells me I can't miss it. Seems like I'm sure to miss it. Do you remember the directions?"

"Not me," Jana said.

"Me neither. Let's walk until we find it."

I stepped into the street, and a horse and wagon almost ran me over.

"What was that about?" I said as I stepped back onto the sidewalk.

A man said, "Can't you see that the sign says not to walk? You can only cross when it says to walk."

The sign changed. People started walking, so Jana and I joined in. We wandered around downtown Albany. Whenever we got to an intersection, we walked in the direction that other people were. We must have walked in circles because I kept seeing many of the same buildings. After what seemed like hours, I stopped and looked up at a sign for the railway station.

"This is it," I said.

"Already?" Jana said.

We walked into the station. It was the largest building I had ever seen. I asked someone where I could buy a ticket to Buffalo. The man pointed to the ticket window. Jana and I walked over, and I asked to buy two tickets to Buffalo.

After paying for the tickets, I asked, "When does the train leave?"

"Oh, don't you know? It leaves in ten minutes. You'll have to hurry. Just follow that hallway to Track 17."

We grabbed our bags and ran. It seemed no matter how much we hurried, there were people in the way. It had to be their job to block our way to the train. We zigged and zagged and didn't knock down too many people. We got to the train just as it was leaving. Jana and I jumped on board the last car before it left the station. We found some seats and sat down.

After about five minutes, a man came by to take our tickets. I handed them to him.

"These tickets are no good," he said.

"We just bought these tickets for Buffalo."

"This train is headed to Boston."

"Is that close to Buffalo?"

He said, "No. This train is going in the opposite direction. You'll have to get off the train."

"But it's moving!" I said.

"I mean at the next stop. You'll have to get off this train and catch a train back to Albany."

"The man said to take the train on Track 17."

"You took the train on Track 18."

"It was close," Jana said.

"Close only counts in dancing," the conductor said.

I had never heard that before. I would learn a lot of new things in America. This is one of them.

CHAPTER 49

FOR BUMS AND STUFF

We got off at the next stop and had to buy two more tickets to get back to Albany.

I asked, "Are my other tickets still good to get to Buffalo."

"Yes. You can even exchange the tickets if you want. Trains leave twice a day. Once in the morning and once at night. You missed the night train, but this train will take you back to Albany tonight. You'll have to find a place to stay and catch the next train in the morning."

We waited at this station for the next train. Some people seemed impatient, but I was used to waiting. When we got on the next train, we made sure it was the right one. Within an hour, we were in Albany again. Then we had to decide where we would spend the night. We could spend money to stay at a hotel. I wasn't sure we had money to spend on something like that.

"Let's go out and see if there's a place where we can sleep outside."

"Sleep outside?"

"Yes, I've done it before. It's not bad, and the weather should be nice."

When we got outside, we saw it had gotten dark already. We walked into a green area. It looked like someone's property, but people walked back and forth through it. I saw a couple kissing right in the open for everyone to see. Things were going to be different in America. We walked across the grass and found a vacant bench.

"Let's sit here and wait until morning," I said.

"Just sit here?"

"We would be sitting on the train anyway."

"Those seats are much more comfortable than this hard bench."

"You're welcome to go back to New York City if you want."

"No, I'm going to Buffalo with you as you had planned."

That hadn't been my plan. My plan from the start had been to go alone. I looked up at the sky and saw the stars. The giant moon rose over the skyline of the city.

I had almost fallen asleep when I felt somebody tapping loudly on the bench.

"Wake up, you two."

I was startled awake and looked up to see a police officer.

"You two can't do that. You'll have to move along," he said.

"We're just sitting here."

"You can't sit here at night. You'll need to find a place to stay. If I catch you sitting here again, I'll have to take you in."

"You mean, arrest us? For sitting?"

"Yes. For sitting."

America was a strange place where a man can be arrested just for sitting.

"What do we do now?" Jana asked.

"It looks like we might have to stay at a hotel after all."

We walked down the street until we found the Curtis Hotel. We walked in and went up to the front desk.

The clerk asked, "Can I help you?"

"We'd like a room."

"For one night?"

"No. Just for a few hours."

"I'm sorry, we're not that kind of place. You'll have to leave."

After we walked out, Jana asked, "What kind of place did he mean?"

"I don't know. I was afraid to ask. There's a lot for me to learn in America."

"Now what?" she said.

"We'll just have to keep walking until the train leaves in the morning."

We walked toward the railway station. We saw what looked like a campfire a few blocks from the station.

"Some people are sitting over there," I said. "Let's go talk to them. Maybe we can join them."

We walked over and found a group of men sitting around a barrel. A fire burned inside. It was a chilly night, so we warmed our hands on the fire. One of the men came over. He wore torn clothes, a dirty cap, and a scruffy beard. His boots had holes in them.

"What's your business here," he asked,

"No business. We need a place to rest for a few hours."

"There are some places to sit over there. Where are you headed?"

I said, "We're going to Buffalo."

"The next train is at six in the morning."

"Yeah, I know."

"I'll tell you the best place to hop on. You'll have to take a running start, though. It speeds up around the bend there."

"A running start?"

"If you want a free ride in one of the empty box cars, you have to run and hop on. If you try to get on when it's standing still, they'll kick you right off that train."

Maybe we could ride free all the way to Minnesota. I needed to save all the money I could for the first winter there. The unused ticket could be traded in for the next train or cash.

I asked Jana, "How fast can you run?"

"As fast as you."

"Are you sure?"

"No way you're losing me. Are we going to chase that train?"

"If these old guys can catch that train, two young ones like us should be able to hop on board."

We rested by the fire for a few hours. A man came by with a jug of whiskey and offered us each a sip. Jana took a sip and grimaced. I could tell she wasn't a whiskey drinker. I took a sip and spat it out.

I must not have been a whiskey drinker either. That was the worst-tasting stuff I had ever had in my whole life. The whiskey tasted like something you'd put in an engine to make it run.

"Don't be wasting that good stuff," he grumbled.

I said, "I'm sorry. It went down the wrong pipe."

I figured there wasn't a right pipe.

CHAPTER 50

THE END OF THE LINE

Soon, the sun came up. The men hurried from their bedrolls and ran to the railway lines. The man we first met stopped to tell us to hurry. When we got to the moving train, he said, "You better move it. These are the last ones. Don't be going all in the same one. Best if you find an empty one."

The train rolled by. He hopped onto an empty car. I saw an empty one and ran toward it. I jumped up into the opening. I wasn't sure if I could help Jana get on board. I looked up, and she was already in the car waiting for me, holding out a hand to help me up.

Jana said, "I thought we were supposed to find an empty one. This doesn't look empty to me."

A man and woman and four children sat huddled in the corner. If looks could have killed, we would have been dead by now. We went to the opposite end of the box car and took the far corner. For about half an hour, we sat staring at each other. Finally, the man got up and came over to us.

"You got any money?" he asked.

"If I had any money, would we be on this boxcar?"

"I guess you're right. I didn't mean to bother you."

He turned and went back to his family. We sat silently for about an hour. One of the kids came over to us.

"I'm supposed to ask you something."

"What are you supposed to ask me?"

"I'm supposed to ask if you got any food on you. We're all so hungry."

I was about to say no, when Jana said, "Yes."

She pulled four slices of bread from a side pocket and handed it to the boy.

He left without a thank you very much. He went over to his corner and shared the bread with his family.

"Where did you get that?" I asked.

"I've had it since we left the ship. I worked in the kitchen, you know. They are still good now. A little hard, but they'll be okay. Do you want some?"

"I thought you gave it away."

"I didn't give all of it away. Here's another slice for you."

She handed me a slice. She was right. It was pretty hard. I hadn't realized how hungry I was until I took a bite of that bread.

"Why didn't you offer me some before?"

"I kept waiting for you to feed me. You never seem to eat for some reason."

Now that I thought about it, I hadn't eaten since the ship. I guess I was just so concerned with getting to where I was going, the thought of eating hadn't occurred to me.

She said, "I got something else. Here's a couple of slices of ham I brought too."

She reached into another pocket and pulled out two slices. I put it on the slice of bread. It made the stale bread taste that much better.

I guess Jana was good to have around, sometimes.

We were jarred awake in the box car as the train slowed. The family sitting in the far corner from us got up.

I asked, "Are we in Buffalo now?"

"You better get off, because this is the end of the line."

The end of the line for him, maybe. Not for me. I had a long way to go yet.

CHAPTER 51

THE END OF THE LINE AGAIN

We got out at the railroad yard along with the other men, women, and families that had gotten a free ride on the train. We had to catch a steamboat next. We found the steamboat ticket office after asking a few directions and getting lost several times. We purchased tickets because I didn't think there was any way we could sneak on board like we had with the train.

When we got to the pier where we were to catch the steamboat, I looked across the water. This lake was as big as the Atlantic! I thought we had made some mistake and had circled back. Upon asking a few people, they said this was Lake Erie, one of the Great Lakes. They named that right. It was a great lake, for sure.

We rode the steamboat across the lake to Detroit.

I liked riding on the steamboat better than the steamship we had used to cross the ocean. I wanted to relax and think, but Jana filled every spare moment with words. One would think she'd run out of words eventually, but she continued on and on.

"We should have stayed in New York. I see Indians over there. Is it safe to be out here?"

I said, "We aren't the first settlers here. Others have gone before us. We should be okay as long as we don't travel too far west. We will be fine as far as we are going."

"I'm glad you think so because I'm not so sure about this."

"Feel free to take the next boat and train back to New York. I won't stop you."

"I'd rather be scared with you than alone in New York."

"How could you be alone in New York? There are millions of people there."

"I don't know any of them."

"You didn't even know me until just a few days ago."

"I know you enough to know I don't want to be with anyone else."

I thought to myself, "How could I be so lucky?"

I was waiting for the steamboat to break down so I would have some excuse to be away from her.

Then we boarded a train headed out west. I had wondered if this day would ever come. I took a seat next to the window and watched the new world pass by. I was amazed at all the trees. More trees than I could imagine. We traveled through small village after small village, and over bridges that passed over rivers.

I thought we would soon run out of land; it just kept coming. America had to be bigger than the Atlantic Ocean.

Eventually, we came to a village. The conductor announced that everyone had to get off. It was the end of the line.

"For me, the end of the line is in Minnesota," I said.

"That's a long way from here. You've reached Elgin. Outside of Chicago."

We needed to get to Dubuque and the Mississippi River, where we would catch the riverboat to Minnesota.

CHAPTER 52

A DOZEN MEN

There were no trains or steamboats, of course, so we had to travel by stagecoach. We went to the stagecoach office and walked up to the clerk.

"When is the next stage for Galena?"

"Galena, just outside of Dubuque, is scheduled to leave in an hour. We might have to cancel this run."

"Why is that?" I asked.

"The drivers who were to make this run have fallen ill. We have no replacements for them."

I looked at Jana, and Jana looked at me.

"I can drive the stagecoach if you are willing to hire me."

"We need two people."

"Jana, here, can help."

"A woman?"

"A woman, yes. But better than any man I have known."

"I don't know. It's a tough ride, even for an experienced driver, across treacherous roads with many dangers along the way. You need someone along with you that can handle a shotgun."

"Jana can do that. She can do anything a man can do. All we need is a map with directions."

"I do have four passengers who are in a hurry to get to Dubuque. I guess you're hired."

He drew a map showing the waystation stops for changes of horses. Passengers could rest and get a meal along the way. An hour later, Jana and I took our positions aboard the stagecoach.

She asked, "Have you ever done this before?"

"No. How hard can it be?"

She looked at me and shook her head. I grabbed the reins and let go of the brake. I snapped the reins. The horses didn't move. I snapped again and shouted for them to move. The horses moved in all different directions, working against each other. It seemed I was doing something wrong. I guess that's how hard it could be.

After a few minutes of getting nowhere fast, Jana grabbed the reins from me and handed the shotgun to me. When I said Jana could do everything, I wasn't wrong. She handled those horses as if she had done it her whole life.

"How'd you learn how to do this?"

"My father made me do a man's work on the farm. He thought I would make a better man than a woman. Can you read the directions?" she asked.

"I can sure try."

We rode along. If we wanted a smooth ride, this wasn't going to be it. I felt every bump on the seat of my pants. At every bump, the passengers in the back screamed, howled, and swore at us. I was sure that when we got off the stagecoach, one or two of them would lynch us from the nearest tree.

Soon, the road got a little better, and the complaining died down. A mile up ahead, I could see a waystation.

"It's about time," I said.

"Yeah, the horses are getting tired. It's time to switch them out. They need their water and their rest."

After we pulled into the station, a young man came out and unhitched the horses and led them off to a corral.

"How long do we stay here?" I asked him.

"As long as it takes. Usually, it's about half an hour. It gives the passengers a chance to have something to eat and drink and do what they need to do. If you know what I mean."

Food and water sounded good to me. We went inside. Jana did her usual expert job of eating. She finished off three times more food than any other passenger or me. She was doing three times the work as me, so it was only fair.

When we got back to the stagecoach, the horses were already hitched. The passengers were waiting on board, complaining about what took us so long.

"What?" Jana asked. "A woman's got to eat, you know."

Someone from inside said, "You eat enough for a dozen men."

Jana said, "I'm worth more than a dozen men."

I wasn't going to argue about that. We got underway. The road had turned bad again. Jana did a better job of avoiding the rough spots. I feared if we hit one of those wrong, we would break an axle or a wheel. Every time we swerved to miss one, I looked over at her and smiled. She looked back and winked at me.

The bad thing happened after the final waystation, about ten miles from Dubuque according to my directions. A few men with masks and guns came *out of the bushes and blocked the road. As I lifted the shotgun to shoot, I heard a gunshot behind me. A bullet missed my head by just a few inches. I heard the bullet whistle past.*

"Get down off the stagecoach. Everybody out. Throw down that shotgun!"

He didn't have to tell me twice. I threw down the shotgun and got off. The grumbling passengers got out. They looked at Jana and me as if we were to blame. I didn't see how it could be our fault that three masked men would hold up the stagecoach at that point.

One of the passengers asked, "Why did you stop?"

I didn't bother answering.

"Empty your pockets. Give us your wallets. All your valuables. Watches and rings," one of the masked men said.

He looked at us and said, "How about you two?"

I said, "We're just poor workers who have no money. That's why we're driving the stagecoach. If we had any money, this is the last thing we would be doing."

I was afraid this would be the last thing we would do. He looked at us and thought about shooting us for having nothing to steal. He just turned away to help the other two pick up the valuables the passengers had thrown to the ground. Then they took the shotgun and backed away into the bushes.

I said to the passengers, "We might as well continue on to Dubuque."

"And then what? We have no money. They took everything we had."

"Now you know what it's like."

"I'll complain at the station to the stagecoach line about this. We'll make sure you're fired."

I said, "They won't have to fire me. After this, driving a stagecoach won't be something that I'll want to do."

"I think you were in cahoots with them, that's what I think. They didn't search you or shoot you."

"If I had been in cahoots with them, I would have left with them. Don't you think?"

He didn't know how to answer that. He got back on board, and we rode the last ten miles into Dubuque. We pulled into the stagecoach office. I was due some money. I didn't even bother collecting. After all, we did get a free ride. I was afraid the passenger would make good on his threat and have us arrested for something we hadn't done.

Jana said, "Here we are in Dubuque. Now what?"

"A riverboat ride. The next stop is Saint Paul in Minnesota."

"Minnesota. Finally. Then what?"

"How do you feel about walking when we get there? I'm not sure how to get from Saint Paul to the Big Woods. That's where my land is that my brother bought for me. We might have to walk."

"How far is that?"

"Forty or fifty miles."

"Forty or fifty miles," Jana said., "I could do that in my sleep."

I thought she probably could.

CHAPTER 53

BANANAS

Our trip to Saint Paul was uneventful as far as the riverboat was concerned. As far as Jana and I were concerned, that was another matter.

After reaching Dubuque, we had to wait six hours to board the boat up the river to Saint Paul. There wasn't much going on at the docks. You can watch not much happening for only so long.

I said, "Let's explore Dubuque. We have some time."

"What's there to see?"

"We won't know until we look."

We walked into downtown Dubuque a few blocks from the docks. There were the usual taverns and hotels. We got to a general store. I had never been in a store like that before. I had never seen so many goods in my life. There were aisles and aisles of canned goods, sugar, flour, and coffee.

"Oh. Look. Pickles. Let's get some," Jana said.

"None for me," I said.

"Why not?"

"I can't stand the smell of them."

Along one side of the store, fruits and vegetables of every kind were stacked in neat rows. I saw one fruit I had never seen before, bananas. I had heard about them but had never eaten any. I just had to buy one. They looked so good, I decided to buy a dozen. I gave half of them to Jana and ate one. It was delicious. I wondered why I had been denied this my whole life.

After two or three, I was getting full and decided to save the bananas for later. Jana had no such plan. She polished all of hers off in one sitting. So I finished all of mine as well. I looked around the store. There were many different kinds of bread, freshly baked. There were tools I had never seen before. People could pick and choose what they wanted, not take the only thing available. Most of what we consumed in Bohemia, we raised ourselves. All the vegetables and fruits came from the fields. Our milk came from our cows. From the pigs, we made bacon and different kinds of sausages. Here, people didn't need to do that. They could just walk into the store and pick out whatever they wanted. Yes. America was the land of plenty.

I must have eaten too many bananas or eaten them too quickly because they didn't agree with me. I had to run out back to the outhouse. I didn't tell Jana. I figured she would know where I went. She was in another aisle looking at women's clothing. I spent quite a bit of time in that outhouse. I was ready to make it my home. When I went back out, I looked around the store for Jana.

I didn't see her. I figured she had probably gone back to the docks alone. Maybe she thought that's where I had gone.

When I got to the riverboat, it was already boarding. I didn't see Jana on the docks. Since I had given her some money, she probably bought a ticket and went on board. It was a good thing that I didn't spend any more time with my friend, the outhouse, or I would have missed the boat.

I boarded with a large group of passengers and found a spot on the lower deck. I figured Jana would be around shortly. I searched the ship, but there was no sign of her. Then the riverboat departed from the docks. We were headed to Saint Paul without Jana!

I stood on the main deck and looked out into the water. That's when I noticed the water was flowing with us, instead of against us. I knew that there was something very wrong with that picture. I approached someone on the main deck.

I asked, "We're going to Saint Paul, aren't we?"

"No, we are headed down the river. To New Orleans, eventually."

"That's the opposite of where I want to go."

I stopped a member of the crew.

"Let me off. I'm going the wrong way."

He said, "No. This boat isn't stopping until we reach Davenport."

"How long will that be?"

"It'll be another hour or so before we stop for more wood, supplies, and passengers."

I stood on the deck and watched Minnesota and Jana drift farther and farther away. I also found that I was missing Jana. After all, what would she do without me? More importantly, I wondered what I would do without her. I had to admit she was a big help. I had grown accustomed to her being at my side.

I got off at Davenport and bought a ticket to Saint Paul. Unfortunately, I had just missed the boat from Davenport back to Dubuque. The next boat to Dubuque wouldn't arrive until the next day.

After I caught the riverboat and arrived in Dubuque, I had a six-hour wait. I got off and looked about the streets for Jana. I even went back to the general store, but she wasn't there. I returned to the riverboat, made sure it was the correct boat this time, and got on board. I looked for Jana but couldn't find her. America was a big place. I didn't know her last name. How would I be able to find her again?

Days later, the riverboat pulled into the docks in Saint Paul. When I exited the boat, I saw her sitting on top of her suitcase. She had a silly grin on her face. After I walked up to her, she stood up and hugged me.

"Vojta, I can't leave you alone for a second. You'll do anything to get away from me."

"I ended up going the wrong way."

"I figured that's what happened to you."

"I don't think the bananas agreed with me. I lost you when I had to go to the outhouse."

She said, "What did you do? Fall in?"

CHAPTER 54

A CROW SINGING

Saint Paul wasn't nearly as large as New York or Chicago. Many of the homes were just shacks built along the river. After I found Jana, I heard some people speaking in Bohemian. I went over to them and asked where they were from. They were from almost the same area in Bohemia that I was from. Only twenty miles away, but twenty miles in Bohemia is a long way.

I asked, "Where are you headed?"

"We are going to live in Saint Paul. We are home. My name is Elena. What's yours?"

"I am Vojta. This is my wife, Jana."

That was the first time I had said that, and it sounded good. I looked over at Jana, who had the biggest smile I had ever seen on her.

"Why are you settling in Saint Paul?" I asked.

"My husband is a shoemaker. There are more people in Saint Paul than in the small towns. The more people, the more shoes. Since most people here walk wherever they go, the shoes wear out. They don't buy new shoes; they repair the old ones."

I said, "There will always be a need for a good shoemaker."

"Are you going to live in Saint Paul?"

"No, we are going to the Big Woods."

"Oh, my! That is a wilderness out there. Nothing but trees. What are you planning to do there?"

"My brother bought me a piece of land. We are going to start a new life."

Jana said, "Maybe we should stay in Saint Paul. It would be a nice place to settle."

"No," I said. "I want to clear the trees and work on land that is mine."

"This man is so stubborn. I've tried to make him see other things. He has his heart set on this Big Woods."

"I wish you luck, but before you start on your journey, how would you like to have a meal with my sister's family? They are expecting us. I'm sure they wouldn't mind a couple more."

I said, "You don't know how much my wife eats."

"Oh, that little thing. How much can she eat?"

"You'd be surprised."

She led the way to her sister's house. There wasn't much traffic, so we didn't have to stop at every corner for a traffic sign telling us when to stop and when to go. I didn't like obeying something like that telling me what to do. We arrived at a plain house on a corner surrounded by trees. People were seated in the yard. When I heard an accordion playing, my spirits lifted. It made me want to dance. I hadn't danced since Bohemia at my sister's wedding.

"Jana, would you like to dance?"

"I thought you'd never ask."

She was full of surprises. I found she was the best dancing partner I'd ever had. She anticipated my every move. It was as if we had been dancing together our whole lives. On this trip, it seemed like we had been together that long.

Then another surprise came. She started singing. She had a beautiful voice. Even though I had heard her talk so much, I didn't think her voice would sound so beautiful in song. She knew all the words. Soon, others joined in.

I found myself with a beer in my hand. Others danced with my wife. I had never seen her so happy. If she got any happier, I would never be able to make her leave this city. We danced to another song. I knew the words, so I joined in.

"Vojta, you are a good man, but you sing like an old crow."

"Next to your singing, anyone would sound terrible!"

"I'm not so sure about that."

Someone said it was time to eat. We sat at a big table. Dumplings and sauerkraut were set out along with pork roast and vegetables of every kind. Elena made sure to keep our plates and beer glasses filled. I saw Elena's eyes grow at how much Jana could eat. With what she ate and all the beer I drank, I was surprised Elena didn't toss us out in the street.

"What are your plans now?" she asked.

"We'll start on our way to the Big Woods."

"First, you must spend the night here. They have a spare bedroom. Actually, it's their son's room. He can sleep on the floor. It won't hurt him for one night."

Elena led us up to the bedroom. After Jana undressed and got into bed, she snuggled close to me. Then we shared our first kiss, a slight peck on the lips. Then the kiss grew more intimate. I couldn't stop myself. Since we were married, as she had often pointed out, we did what married couples did. We enjoyed each other.

I loved everything about her. She was soft to the touch. I enjoyed every caress. I had been with women before. This time, it seemed different. This was meant to be. It made me wonder why I had waited so long. It would have made the long journey that much easier.

The following day, we woke up to the smell of frying bacon and coffee brewing. When we got downstairs, Elena looked at us. We must have had silly grins on our faces.

She said, "Someone enjoyed their night, I see."

How did women know these things? As we ate breakfast, I told her some of the stories of our journey.

She said, "I'm envious. My trip was boring. Nothing happened. It was just boring riding, riding, riding, riding. Changing from boats to trains and trains to boats. You are so lucky to have had such adventures on the way."

I said, "Our adventures are just beginning. Right, Jana?"

"If my life is full of these adventures, I won't be bored. That's for sure."

CHAPTER 55

MY BABIES

We had planned to walk to the Big Woods, however, Elena told us of a ferryboat down the river to the Sand Creek Landing. I had heard my brother talk of that landing.

When we reached the dock, we saw it was under a foot of water from the Mississippi. Jana and I waded through the swift current and boarded the ferry.

The ferryman said, "Hello, folks. You can call me Ike. Just to warn you, this could be a rougher trip than usual."

"It seems like a nice enough day," I said.

"About the nicest that you'll get here in Minnesota," Ike said.

"What's the problem then?"

"The snow is melting and flowing into the Minnesota River. When we get there, you'll see the river's over the banks and moving a lot faster. It will be like we're going uphill."

"Is it safe to go?" I asked.

"It's as safe as it's going to be. That's all I can say."

Which wasn't saying much.

Jana said, "We aren't going to let something as little as this stop us."

It turned out we were the only two people brave enough to make this trip. Jana and I weaved our way around flour, building materials, and farm equipment, and sat in the only vacant spot on the ferry.

"Hang on!" Ike said as we pulled away from the dock. We were hit with a huge wave, but it was nothing compared to what we had encountered on the trip across the ocean.

He was right about it being a slow trip. It did seem like we were going uphill. We passed buildings on the shore that were under water. We even saw a cow tied to a fence post, her feet in the river.

"That poor cow," Jana said. "Let's stop and help it."

"I'd love to," Ike said. "Once we got there, we'd never get out. We'd be stranded as much as the cow is now. I don't see it getting much higher than this, so the cow should be okay."

I guessed Ike was trying to make Jana feel better about abandoning the cow. As we went along, we met another house, not on shore but floating in the water. The three people on board, a man and two children, were perched upon the highest point of the roof. The children were crying, and the man held his head in his hands. They took no notice of us as we passed.

"They're getting a free trip to wherever they're going," Ike said.

Jana said, "It's away from where they want to be."

"That could be," Ike said. "That could be."

Around a bend up ahead, we heard screams and someone shouting for help. We came upon a woman hanging on a fallen tree that had floated down the river. It was caught in other debris near the shore. There wasn't a way for her to make it to safety.

Jana said, "A cow is one thing. A woman is another. We have to save her."

"I guess I can slow down and come to sort of a stop next to her," Ike said. "One of you will have to toss this rope out and see if you can help her."

I grabbed the rope. As we neared the woman in the tree, I tossed the rope to her. It missed her by twenty feet.

"Give me that rope," Jana said.

I handed it to her. She twirled it and tossed it toward the woman. It was a direct hit.

"Great throw," Ike said.

After the woman tied the rope around her waist, we pulled her toward the ferry. A few times, she went under due to the heavy flow of the water against her. Finally, we got her up next to the ferry. I grabbed one arm, Jana the other, and we lifted her out of the water. She collapsed on the deck, gasping for breath.

"I hope she didn't take on too much water," I said.

"It was either that or she would just drown right where she was," Jana said.

We tried to revive the woman as the ferry headed toward Sand Creek.

"I don't know the first thing about this," I said.

"Neither do I," Jana said.

All we could do was watch, hope, and wait for her to catch her breath, which she soon did.

"My babies!" she said. "My husband! My babies! They're back at the tree. Did you save them?"

"We didn't see anyone else by the tree," I said.

"You've got to go back!"

Ike said, "I don't have time to be going back."

"But my babies!" she said.

She got up and looked back to where she had been by the tree. She jumped in the water and floated towards where we picked her up. The speed of the water took her past the fallen tree. We watched as she disappeared down the river.

"There's no way we can catch her," Ike said.

"What about her children?" Jana asked.

"I didn't see any there, did you?" Ike asked.

"No. I didn't either," I said.

"Maybe they all drowned," Jana said.

"If they did, she'll be joining them," Ike said.

"They were probably the ones we saw on the house," I said.

"I hope so," Jana said. "Maybe it's her family, and she can meet up with them when they get to Saint Paul."

"You think so?"

Jana said, "If she doesn't, I don't want to know about it."

As we fought the current, which seemed to have gotten stronger, the water encroached upon the Big Woods.

"I don't know how we're going to do this," Ike said. "We're almost to Sand Creek."

"That's a good thing, isn't it?" I asked.

"Yes. Except the dock is under water. I don't know how we're going to get near the landing. And if we do, how will you get ashore? I'm going to have to turn back."

I said, "We've come this far. We're not turning back."

"I'm not getting any closer to shore than this."

"Can you get us in just a little bit closer?" Jana asked.

"Jana and I will jump off and swim to shore."

"I can't let you do that."

"You're not letting us do anything. We're doing it," Jana said.

He said, "I can't take any responsibility for this."

"Just get us as close as you can. Are you ready for this, Jana?"

She was already in the water swimming towards shore, using her bag to help her stay afloat. I decided to do the same thing. The current took us away from Sand Creek. As we neared the Big Woods, the current seemed to slow. We were able to kick our way into the Big Woods. We each grabbed onto a tree and held on to rest.

"Now what, Vojta?"

"I hope we can make it to dry land from here."

"Grab on to this," a man shouted.

He was about twenty feet away on shore. The rope landed close to Jana. She grabbed onto it, and a man pulled her next to where he was standing.

"Now, your turn."

After he pulled me to shore, he said, "I saw you jump off that ferry. It's braver than anything I would ever have done."

I said, "We had no choice. It was either that or head back to Saint Paul."

"Anything but that," he said. "After you've gotten this far. By the way, did you happen to see a house float down the river?"

"It was hard to miss," Jana said.

"That's my brother's house. He, his wife, and two kids were on top of the house."

"It was just a man and two kids," I said. "We tried to rescue the wife. She jumped back into the water for her children."

"That's something she would do. Trust me. That's the kind of woman she is."

I looked over to Jana, and I thought that was the kind of woman Jana was.

CHAPTER 56

MY BROTHER'S PLACE

We left Sand Creek Landing and headed toward Plum Creek.

"Now, to see my brother. It will be easy to find him. He said if you follow Plum Creek, you can't miss it. He has a house by the creek near my new homestead. He told me if I got lost, just ask anyone. They know him. They can point me in the right direction."

We started walking along the creek. We found that was an uneasy task. Following the creek was impossible due to heavy brush, reeds, and swamps. We had to find a different way. So we went back to where we had started. We discovered we had only walked half a mile. It seemed like we had been walking ten.

Back at the landing, we saw a team of horses and a wagon dropping off lumber to be loaded onto the next ferry to Saint Paul. I expected Jana to ask if she could go along with the lumber, but she didn't. We walked up to the man who had saved us from the river.

The man said, "I'm picking up supplies over there. I don't know where you want to go. Maybe I could give you a ride."

"Do you know where Nova Praha is?" I asked. "That's where my brother lives. His name is Lukas Sitec. Perhaps you know him."

It looked like he did, but he answered, "Can't say as I do."

"Can you give us directions?"

"I'm headed that way myself. Would you like a ride? I can't let you ride up front because my wife will be here shortly, and she'll sit up front with me. You can go in the back of the wagon."

"If you knew of some of the places we've ridden on our journey, you would know that this would be a luxury for us."

Soon, his wife came with her provisions, and we were on our way. I don't know how the man knew his way. If we had tried to follow any directions along this route, we would have ended up back in New York City. That would have made Jana happy.

We wound around and over the creek many times. We passed land that was mostly wooded. Every once in a while, we would see a shack with smoke coming out of the chimney. The farmers were hard at work cutting wood, laying in for the winter early. I wished I was in their position. I was going to be a day late and a dollar short.

I told Jana what I was thinking.

"Now you have me to help. It will go five times faster."

I don't know how she calculated, but she was probably right.

The driver of the wagon looked back at us and said over his shoulder, "We are almost there. We can let you off short of town. We have to go in the other direction."

After thanking him, we headed down the main street. I knew if you wanted to find someone in town, you went to the nearest tavern. I didn't see Lukas sitting anywhere in the bar when we went in. We went up to the bartender and ordered a couple of beers. I took a sip. Beer sure tasted different here. I wondered if it was some different recipe or the water. Even after I drank the whole glass of beer, I didn't feel a thing.

When the bartender returned with my change, I asked him if he knew my brother and where he lived.

"Oh, Lukas. That no-good?"

"What do you mean?"

"He owes everybody in town."

"He does? He told me he has a place of his own."

"Yes, he has a place of his own. It's probably in some ditch somewhere."

I said, "We have to find him. He bought some land for me in the Big Woods by Plum Creek. I sent him the money."

"If you sent him money, I'm betting it's gone."

"That can't be. That just can't be."

I looked over at Jana. She had a look on her face. It was an 'I told you so' look even though she hadn't told me so.

I asked the bartender, "Where can I find my brother?" "I'm not sure. You might check with the blacksmith."

CHAPTER 57

GO HOME

We found the blacksmith shop at the end of town. As we neared the entrance, we could smell the hot coals. We saw the blacksmith using a hammer to pound a hot piece of iron on his anvil. When he saw us, he didn't stop. As the old saying goes, you had to strike when the iron was hot.

When he finished, he looked up at us and said, "If you need anything fixed, it'll be the end of the week."

"No, it isn't that," I said.

"What then?"

He wiped his sweaty face with his dirty hands and dirtied his face even more than it had been before.

"I don't have time to be wasting," he said.

"We're looking for my brother, Lukas. Someone said he might be here."

"Oh, him. Now, you're wasting my time, for sure. He's out back. Just go around the corner."

He went back to heating another piece of iron on the coals. Jana and I headed out toward the back of the blacksmith shop. We walked through the tall weeds to the rear of the building. We found a tiny porch with the door open. We looked inside and saw Lukas asleep on a small bed covered with filthy sheets and a stained pillow. There was no other furniture on the porch or pictures on the wall. However, many empty bottles of whiskey were strewn about. Lukas woke up and looked up at us when we came in.

"Vojta! What are you doing here?"

"I told you I was coming."

"You shouldn't have. You should have let me know. I would have told you."

"What would you have told me?" I asked.

"It's good to see you anyway. You are looking good."

"I wish I could say the same for you."

"Who is this with you?"

"This is Jana. My wife."

"Ah, your wife, and you don't tell me. Is she from our town?"

"No. I met her on the voyage to get here."

"Yeah, you always have been lucky."

"What would you have warned me about?"

"For one thing, I would have told you there is nothing for you here."

"Nothing for me? What about my land? I sent you money to buy some land for me here."

"Oh, that."

"Yes, that."

"There is no land."

"Didn't you buy it?"

"No. I lost the money."

"You lost it?"

"I thought with your money that you'd have a piece of land. If I could double it, then I could have a piece of land too. We both could be wealthy landowners here in Minnesota."

"In the letters, you said you bought my land."

"I shouldn't have written those letters to you. I never thought you would come."

"What did you think I would do? Just send you money for nothing?"

"Do what you want with me. You couldn't feel any worse than I do right now."

"I wouldn't bet on that. It was all the money I had. What am I to do now that I'm here?"

"I don't know what to say. There is work out in the fields, helping farmers on their land. Putting their crops in and help harvest at the end of the season. You can save up enough money to make it through the winter."

"Here I am again, working for another farmer. All my hard work is going to someone else. I could have done that in Bohemia."

"I don't know what to say."

"You should say you'll get my money back."

"I can't. This is where I live. He lets me stay here. I do odd jobs for him. It's just a bed, as you can see. I do all the work that he doesn't care to do."

"You have enough to buy whiskey and get drunk," Jana said.

"I sweep out the bars, and they give me money for that."

"Why didn't you buy food? Look at you. You've lost weight," I said.

"I'm about half the man I used to be."

"In more ways than one."

Jana said, "What are we to do, Vojta? You said there would be land here and it would be ours."

"Yes, I know. What am I to do, Lukas?"

Lukas said, "Like I told you. Farmers around here need help. I would work myself, but I'm too weak. You look strong. Between you and Jana, you could help them and earn enough money to make it back to Bohemia."

"Go back to Bohemia! After all I've done to get here. All we've done. Now I must go to work for someone else."

"If you don't go back, you could at least make enough to survive the winter," Lukas said.

"Where am I supposed to find this farmer to work for? Do they magically drop out of the sky?"

"Go to the tavern and ask around. They will know of farmers who need help. Just don't tell them I'm your brother."

"That's the last thing I'll do. You can be sure of that. Because I have no brother. Come on, Jana. Let's go."

Before we turned our backs to leave, we saw Lukas pull another bottle of whiskey from under his bed. He took two healthy swallows, curled up, and fell asleep.

CHAPTER 58

LOST IN THE BIG WOODS

Our next stop was a tavern. There seemed to be many of those. At the first tavern, we asked the bartender if he knew where we might find work. He said, "I don't know. You might ask those two men over there."

We walked over and said, "We are looking for work. Someone who needs farm laborers. We can help put in crops and help in the fields and help with chores."

"We have barely enough to keep us busy," one of the men answered. "You'll find no work around here, I can tell you that."

"Are there any jobs for a good mechanic?"

"There are more mechanics here than we know what to do with."

At each tavern, the response was the same.

"This isn't a good start," Jana said. "We should go back to New York."

"No. I'm in Minnesota and this is where I'll stay."

She said, "Then I think we should go to church and pray."

"I didn't know you were religious."

"There's a lot about me you don't know."

"I guess I have a lot of time to learn."

"In our village, the priest knew everything about everyone."

That's one thing about Jana. She was always right. We walked to the church and went inside. It was empty except for a priest who was tending to the altar. He was an older man with gray hair. His hair and white collar were soiled and in need of washing. The church looked like it had been having a hard time of it.

Jana walked up to him and said, "We're a newly married couple. We are looking for work to make it through the winter. Do you know of any farmers who need help?"

He said, "I know of a farmer named Steckman. He was in here last week looking for someone. I can tell you where his farm is. He still might need help in his fields. I would check with him."

"How do we find him?"

"He is eight miles out of town to the east in the Big Woods. Just follow the old cart path through the woods."

We thanked him and headed out of town. Following the cart path wasn't as easy as the priest had told us it would be. It disappeared at times, and we walked around looking for it again to find where it continued. As we wandered around, we noticed we were headed back west to where we had started. At times, we saw footprints that we had made. We were going around in circles and had no idea where we were going. Soon, it was night, and we had to sleep. We found an old hollow log that looked big enough for both of us to crawl into. Jana went in first. I edged my way in next to her.

We tried to sleep. Ants and other pests crawled over us, interrupting our sleep. Finally, I crawled out, followed closely by Jana.

"What now?" she asked.

"We need to build a fire. Get some kindling, and I'll find some firewood. I've got matches."

Soon, we had a good fire going. We sat next to it to warm up. I don't know how long we were sitting there when I heard something or someone rustling in the bushes. If it was a bear, I wasn't sure what to do. We had no weapons. I knew that climbing a tree wasn't an option. I stuck a piece of wood into the flames and set the end of it on fire. Maybe the fire would keep it away.

"What are you doing here?" a man said from the darkness.

"It's cold out. We're trying to keep warm," I said.

"You're trying to set my woods on fire is what you're trying to do."

"We're trying to get to Steckman's place eight miles away, and we got turned around. This is where we ended up."

"I know him. What do you want to see him for?"

"We wanted to know if he was looking for someone to help him on the fields. We are good laborers, and we need work."

"You won't find it from him."

Jana and I looked at each other, each of us dejected.

The man said, "I'm looking for help. If you don't set my woods on fire, maybe I could use you."

I quickly stamped out the fire.

"That's better," he said. "What kind of work can you do?"

"We both used to work on farms in Bohemia."

"Ah, so you can work hard."

"Yes, we can."

"What are you doing coming to America with no money?"

"That's a long story."

"I'm not interested in any long stories. I'm just interested in some people who will work hard."

"We'll work for you for a place to sleep, some food, and money to help us make it through the winter."

"That I can probably do. You'll have to sleep in the barn along with the cows and pigs."

"We don't mind that. They'll help keep us warm, along with a blanket and something soft to sleep on."

CHAPTER 59

AND THEN THERE WAS LIDDY

The man, who was about six feet tall and lean with dark hair and eyes, told us his name was Hanzel. We followed him through the woods until we came to a cabin. Next to it stood a barn that looked like it was in better shape than the cabin.

He said, "I suppose you need something to eat now."

"We haven't eaten since Saint Paul."

"Then you must be starving. This is the only free meal you get out of me. After this, you will work for what you get. I'll work you hard too because we have plenty to do. In addition to the chores and the fieldwork, I want to clear trees for more plowable land. So I will need you to help me take down trees."

"I can do that."

"What will she do?"

"Like I've always said. Jana can do the work of a dozen men."

"From the looks of it, she can eat like a dozen men."

Jana had already finished one plate and was on her second.

"I've never seen a little woman like her eat so much."

"That she does. She'll outwork any man; I tell you that."

A woman stomped into the kitchen. I knew it couldn't be, but she looked half as tall as Hanzel and weighed half again as much.

"Who are these two now?"

"This is my wife Liddy. They're going to help me in my work."

"What do we need them for? You can do it by yourself. It looks like they're eating us out of house and home."

"It will be okay. I need the help."

"They'll take advantage of you, more than likely."

"They are from Bohemia, and they need help."

"They should have stayed in Bohemia."

Liddy turned to stomp away.

"Do you have a couple of blankets for them?"

"Now, they want blankets. I'm sure when we wake up in the morning, our blankets will be gone and whatever else they can take from the barn."

I said, "You can trust us."

"I have seen this many times before," she said. "Trust. We have no reason to trust you."

Hanzel said, "I'm going to take a chance on them. Okay?"

"You might say it's okay. It's not okay by me."

She turned and walked away. A few minutes later, she threw two blankets into the kitchen, that landed at our feet.

Hanzel said, "I think it'll be fine. If it hadn't been, she wouldn't have given you the blankets."

CHAPTER 60

IT'S NOT MUCH

The next day, we were put to work. It was a hard day. We got up when the sun got up. We helped with the chores, milked the cows, and fed the chickens.

Hanzel said, "I want to take down some trees by the north pasture."

I looked toward the pasture. One or two trees had been taken down. He had a long way to go before it would be fit for plowing.

"Do you have any crops already planted?"

"Yes, the fields to the south have been planted with corn and wheat. Liddy has started a garden with potatoes to get us through the winter."

I said, "Let's get to work on those trees."

I grabbed an axe and saw and headed out there. Jana did the same.

Hanzel said, "Wait for me. I'll tell you which ones I want to keep."

Between Jana and I, it took about an hour to take one tree down and trim the branches off the log. The stump might be left in the ground for a few years to let it deteriorate. Eventually, the stump had to be grubbed. A grub ax, 4 to 8 inches wide and flat on one side, would be used to dig around stumps and to cut off small roots. A pickaxe would be used to cut off larger roots. A double-bit or pickaxe had two sides. It was used to break hardened or rocky soil and chop roots while loosening the soil.

I could see why he only had a few trees done. It would be many summers before he could make a decent field out of these woods. Hanzel needed our help to get it done.

"How did you get the south pasture done so quickly," I asked.

"Lucky, I guess," he said. "That land was grassland with not many trees. That's why I picked this spot. It's by the creek. The trees I did take down, I used to build the cabin and the barn."

"How long have you been here?"

"We've been here five years. I had no help at all with the building of the house and barn. It was just my hard work."

"You made it through the winters."

"Winters here are a lot colder than in Bohemia. A lot more snow. There's nothing to do except go out and tend to the cattle and then get back to the house to keep warm for the rest of the day. We have kerosene lamps so I can read books. Just my wife to talk to."

I looked at Jana and said, "If you want someone to talk to, there she is. Right there. She could talk your ear off if you let her."

"Well, I need my ears, so I'll pass on that. Maybe you could work on my wife. She doesn't listen to me anyway, so she doesn't need ears."

We all laughed at that.

We worked hard for the rest of the day and took down four trees. After that, Liddy warmed up to us. She brought lunches and water to us during the day. We even saw a smile on her face.

"I didn't think she was capable of it," Hanzel said. "I haven't seen her smile for five years."

I said, "A happy wife makes for a happy life."

"Maybe I can have a happy life now," Hanzel said.

We worked hard throughout that whole summer. We earned our keep. I didn't know what Hanzel was going to pay us. I hoped he hadn't forgotten about that. We had never agreed on any wage. If he asked Liddy about it, I'm sure we wouldn't get anything.

After the fall harvest, it seemed like Hanzel had done well. We could see winter was about to come in. The cold winds blew from the north, and temperatures dropped.

Hanzel said, "Your work here is done. I can't keep you here through the winter."

"That'll be just fine. If you pay us, we will be on our way," I said.

Hanzel agreed. However, Liddy overheard this.

"With all the food that woman eats, you owe them nothing. If you ask me, they should pay you."

"But I agreed to pay them."

"You will not pay them. Send them on their way. We have done all we can for them."

Hanzel looked at us apologetically. My mistake was bringing this up in front of Liddy. He ordered us off the farm. Or rather, Liddy did.

As we marched down the road, Jana said, "What now?"

Around the corner, we saw Hanzel. He waved us over from the woods.

He said, "It's not much. It's all I could get."

He handed us a few dollars plus a rifle and some ammunition.

That wouldn't last us very long.

CHAPTER 61

THE HOLE IN THE WALL

We left Hanzel's farm and looked to the west. We saw storm clouds looming over the horizon. The temperature had dropped about twenty degrees. After we had walked for an hour, it had fallen to thirty-two degrees. Freezing.

Jana looked at me and said, "This doesn't look good. At least they could have given us something to eat before we left."

"That would have been too much for Liddy. And after everything we did for them too. Just for meals and a roof over our heads."

"I would gladly welcome a meal and a roof over my head right now. What are we going to do?"

"We have a rifle. If you see any game out there, a rabbit or a squirrel, it will be food for the night."

"We'll need shelter," she said. "Maybe we'll come upon an abandoned cabin somewhere."

"We'd have better luck finding that log that we tried to sleep in the first day we were here."

"Look," she said. "A rabbit."

I picked up the rifle, aimed, and shot. I succeeded in scaring the rabbit and shooting an old oak tree that was nowhere near the rabbit.

I said, "I'm not so good at this."

"You're not unless we plan on eating the bark off that tree. Hand that rifle to me."

Soon, we spotted another rabbit. She lifted the rifle, took aim, and shot it. There was nothing this woman couldn't do.

"At least we won't starve."

"Today anyway."

"Do you know how to skin a rabbit?" I asked.

She looked at me with an 'of course I do look' and said, "What do you think? It's a good thing I borrowed a knife when we left Hanzel's."

As we walked along, a few snowflakes floated out of the sky. Within minutes, it turned into a heavy snowfall. A half-hour later, the wind picked up, and we were in the middle of a blizzard. We could barely see ten feet in front of us.

"Yes, we won't starve," Jana said. "We'll freeze to death out here instead."

Finally, we found ourselves in a gully. It was a dead end. I was afraid we would be walking around in circles again. I looked to my left and saw an opening in the rocks in the gully.

"Jana, look there. Perhaps that is a cave where we could take cover."

We moved over to the cave and entered, hoping that no wild animals had also taken shelter there. At least we had the rifle, and Jana was a good shot. Unless it happened to be a bear, we'd be okay. The cave opened into a wide-open area.

"I wonder how far back this goes," I said.

"I don't know. It's impossible to see," she said.

"Let's build a fire right here and warm up. I'll hunt up some firewood and kindling."

While I went to search for that, Jana skinned the rabbit. At least, we would eat. We would be warm under the cover of the cave. After we ate, I grabbed one of the lighted pieces of firewood. It gave off enough light to illuminate the back of the cave, where I saw a tunnel.

"Jana, look here. This cave stretches way back. Let's see where this goes."

With our dim light, we walked into the darkness. We came to several dead ends and ended back where we started. We continued searching and came to a huge area, larger than the living room of Hanzel's cabin.

I said, "Look, Jana. It's warmer here. A guy could live in here."

"Don't you be getting any ideas. I'm not staying here."

"We might not have a choice. We might have to spend the winter here."

"What are we going to sleep on?"

"Just the dirt floor," I said. "I consider ourselves lucky. We could be out there freezing. Here we have warmth. We have a fire. We have shelter. We can go out and hunt for food. I think we'll be okay."

She said, "Yes. What happens when the baby comes?"

"Baby?"

"I haven't told you. I'm pregnant."

"How long?"

"About three months."

"Why didn't you tell me?"

"There never was a good time."

A father? I was going to be a father! In the middle of Minnesota. With no job. No roof over our heads except this cave and about to bring a baby into the world. But it would be our baby. Talk about starting out with almost nothing.

"Now what?" she asked, her favorite line.

"You sit here by the fire. I'll try to find something to make a bed. So we don't have to sleep on the dirt floor tonight."

I went out in the middle of the blizzard and found leaves piled at the end of the gully. I removed my coat, scooped armfuls into it, and carried it back into the cave. It would take more than that. I made about a dozen or more trips out there. Soon, we had a pile of leaves in the corner of the cave.

She said, "It's a good thing I kept these blankets. If Liddy had known that I had borrowed them, she never would have let us get off the farm with them."

I told her to make a bed for us to sleep on. I again went out in the blizzard and found more wood from fallen trees in the gully. After several trips, we had a pile of firewood drying next to the fire in our smoked-filled shelter.

She said, "It looks like we're okay for now."

"We've been through worse."

"Yes," she said. "And it looks like we might be in for even worse yet."

"We'll make it, Jana. We always have. We always will."

I was waiting for her to say something about being better off if we had stayed in New York. She would be right. I didn't know my worthless brother was going to squander the money for my land. If he hadn't done that, we would have been all set for the winter. We would be in our cabin with potatoes that we would have planted in a garden.

I said, "Jana, did you notice? We are next to a creek?"

"I did notice that."

"There might be fish in there," I said.

"How good are you at fishing?" she asked.

"I've never done it. How hard could it be?"

"As hard as shooting a rifle."

CHAPTER 62
SO THAT IS MAREK

We had been living in the cave for a couple of weeks. It wasn't all that bad. The pile of leaves made sleeping more comfortable than lying on the bare ground. Each day, I would go out and scrounge up firewood. I soon had a stack of wood in the cave large enough to last a month in case another blizzard came up. Fortunately, none had. Jana hunted each day and finally shot a deer. She knew how to dress it. We had enough meat to last us until the firewood ran out.

One day while searching for firewood, even though we didn't need it, I heard a voice.

"What are you doing out here?"

I was so startled that I turned around and dropped my armful of wood. I couldn't answer. I didn't know what to say.

He asked again, "What are you doing out here?"

"Looking for wood."

"Yes, I can see that. I've heard shooting out here. I figured someone was living on my land. I thought I'd find out what was going on."

I finally had to admit it.

"My wife and I are living in that gully over there. In a cave."

"You're what?"

"Yes, we're living in that cave over there."

"Why are you living in there?"

"We had no other place to live. A blizzard came, and we needed shelter. That cave is where we ended up."

"I don't believe it," he said.

"Would you like to come and see for yourself?"

"Show me."

He followed me into the opening. Jana was leaning over the fire preparing a meal.

The man said, "I'll be. If I hadn't seen it, I wouldn't have believed it. You know, I still don't believe it."

"My name is Vojta. This is Jana," I said.

"I'm Marek."

"We had hoped to have our own place," I said.

"That didn't happen," Jana added. "We worked for Hanzel last summer. He was supposed to pay us, but that didn't happen either."

"Hanzel's okay, but that wife of his," I said, shaking my head. "If it had been up to Hanzel, we would have been paid. We wouldn't be living here in this cave."

Jana said, "Would you like some food? We have plenty."

"I would love some," Marek said. "I've been living on beans. I've tried hunting. I'm not so good at it. So it's coffee and beans. Beans and coffee."

I said, "I would love some coffee. I haven't had any since we left Saint Paul."

"Next time I stop by, I'll bring you some."

"You mean we can stay here?" Jana asked.

"Sure. Why not? I feel bad that I have nothing better to offer you."

"This cave will work just fine," I said.

"I've lived here a couple of years, trying to get my farm going. Since you worked for Hanzel all summer, I know you're good workers. If you need work in the summer, I'll gladly hire you."

"Both of us?" I asked. Then I again went into the spiel about Jana being a harder worker than most men.

He said, "It's a deal."

He looked over at the makeshift bed we had in the corner.

"Is that where you're sleeping?"

"Yes," Jana said. "It's comfortable enough."

He looked over at Jana and said, "If you don't mind me asking, are you going to have a baby?"

Jana said, "Yes. We're going to have a boy. We're going to have Vojta's son."

"I don't know how you know that," Marek said, "but more power to you. I tell you what. I have this old mattress. You're welcome to it. Before you say anything, I must tell you, though. It used to be a bed for my dog before he passed away."

Jana said, "Thank you. If it was good enough for your dog, it will be good enough for us."

"You're welcome," Marek said with a smile. "I sure miss that dog. He was good company out here."

Jana said, "If we can stay here, you are welcome anytime."

"Is there anything else you need?"

"No," I said. "You've done more than enough."

"A book," Jana interrupted. "The thing I would like is to read a book. I haven't read a book since Bohemia. I know it doesn't seem like much. It would help pass the time."

"Books. My goodness. You're talking to the right person. I have more books than I know what to do with. When I bring the mattress, I'll bring you some books to read."

"In exchange for a meal," Jana said.

"Yes, in exchange for a good meal. You know what else you need? You need some light. If you're going to read, you need some candlelight."

"We have no money for candles," I said.

"That's another thing I have plenty of. When I go to the store, I make sure to buy candles. I will bring you some. So you aren't living in the dark here."

Each day he had brought more books and pieces of furniture he said he didn't need. One day, Jana was reading a book Marek had given her. She looked up at me and said, "Things are looking up for us."

I said, "Yes. We have it pretty good."

Suddenly she had a pained look on her face.

"What's the matter?"

"Nothing," she said. "I have to go outside."

When she came back, her face was wet with tears. She had been crying. I'd never seen her cry before. She always talked so much that she didn't have time to cry. No matter what happened, she had a smile on her face. The smile was gone from her face now.

"What's wrong, Jana?"

"I can't talk about it."

"What happened? You have to tell me."

"I can't talk about it."

She got onto the dog's mattress and curled up into a ball and cried herself to sleep. The following day, when I came back with the firewood, I found her preparing a meal. I thought things would be back to normal, but she didn't have anything to say.

I asked her, "What happened?"

"You don't want to know."

"I do. Tell me."

"I lost the baby."

"You did? You lost the baby?"

"Yes, I'm a failure. I lost your son."

Tears came to my eyes. I had so wanted a son. Even a daughter. Most of all, it hurt me that she was hurting and that she was sad.

I said, "These things happen."

"Not to me they don't."

I believed that. She was so good at so many things. In this one thing she wanted so much, more than anything else, she felt she had failed.

"It's not your fault. It's us living in this cave. That's what did it."

She said, "I'm made from tougher stuff than that. Things could have been a lot worse. Living here had nothing to do with what happened. It's me."

She put the food in front of me but didn't set anything for herself. That was unusual for someone who could eat so much. She turned away, went back to bed, and curled up into a ball.

CHAPTER 63

HOPE

For days, she lay there. Not eating. Not talking. The silence was almost more than I could bear. I tried talking, but it couldn't fill the void of her losing our child.

When the next blizzard came, she stood and looked out of the opening in the cave. She just stared out there for the longest time.

Finally, she said, "I think I will go out and hunt."

That brought my hopes up. When she left, I picked up the book I had been reading. I looked up occasionally for her to come back. I didn't know how long she was gone. Then I noticed our rifle sitting in the corner. I walked into the blizzard to look for her. The snow had obliterated all her tracks.

I searched around the gully and didn't see her. I decided to walk into the woods. The snow came down harder and harder. I couldn't wander too far away from the cave. I might not find my way back. After an hour of searching, I decided to head back to the cave to see if she had come back. There was no Jana.

Soon it got dark and the blizzard got even worse. I couldn't see out of the opening in the cave. There was still no sign of Jana. If I had wanted to go out in the blizzard, I wouldn't be able to see anything. I had to wait until morning.

By dawn, the snow had let up. I ventured out when the sun first came up. I hadn't slept all night. If there had been any tracks, they were long gone now. I widened my search. I went a mile in each direction. I didn't find her anywhere.

Occasionally, I would head back to the cave, hoping she had found her way back. I always came back to an empty cave.

Every night, I sat in the cold, dark, empty cave. I didn't even bother lighting a fire. What was the use? For days and days, I continued the search with the help of Marek. There was no Jana.

After a month had passed, I realized that Jana was gone. Things would have been different if I hadn't been so stubborn about settling in Minnesota.

My only hope was she had made her way out of the woods and was on her way back to New York, the place she wanted to be. I had to hope she made it out of the Big Woods and made it to New York City. A place she hadn't wanted to leave.

Then I found myself believing it because I didn't want to believe the other horrible thought that would come to my mind. That she was lying dead somewhere in the fields or the Big Woods. That she had died in the blizzard that day.

CHAPTER 64

ONE MORE TRY

I decided to go out again. I didn't know if I would find her, but I had to try. Sitting in this cave, day after day and night after night, and not knowing what happened to Jana was too much for me. I couldn't take another day of it.

Marek had given up on the search. He told me that Jana was either dead or had gone back to New York. How could she go back to New York City without me? The loss of our son had changed her. She wasn't the same woman who made the voyage with me across the ocean.

We should have stayed in New York. I would have had the perfect job there. What was I thinking? I could be a farmer, but I was better suited to be a mechanic. It took a winter in Minnesota for me to find that out.

It was starting to snow again. When didn't it? It was always snowing. Jana had been right all along. We should have stayed in New York. We would have been happy there. Then again, I might have always wondered what would have happened if I had gone to Minnesota.

Now I know.

I will try one more time. When I get back, I hope to write in this journal that I have found Jana. That we will be happy again. That we will go to New York as she had wanted all along.

If I don't find her, I'll go to New York to search for her. In a city of two million people, it will be impossible to find her. I have to try.

PART THREE: THE SOLUTION - 1963

CHAPTER 65

YOU CAN'T KNOW EVERYTHING

After I finished reading the journal, I said, "I don't think we have to turn this skull over to the sheriff. I think we found out who this skull belongs to."

"I agree."

"Besides, did you notice?" I asked. "I was wrong. There is no hole in the skull."

"There's just a lot of dirt in that spot. I can see how you would think it was a hole," she said.

"It took over a hundred years, but we found her."

"This has to be Jana. She was buried up there in that field all these years. She must have gotten lost in the blizzard."

"I agree with you. Even if we took the skull to the sheriff, he'd never be able to trace it back to Jana," I said.

Rachel said, "I wonder if Vojta made it to New York."

"We could go to New York and see if we can find Vojta. What happened to him? There's got to be some record."

"Going to New York. That's a pretty big deal. My folks would never let me do that."

"Neither would mine," I said. "Plus, it would cost a lot of money. And we can't hitchhike."

"Maybe when we're older, we can find out what happened to him."

I said, "I guess we'll never know the answer to the boot with no sole and new shoelaces."

"We can't expect to know everything."

"I suppose you can't know everything until after high school," I said.

We sat in the dim candlelight of the cave. I looked at Rachel. I could see tears in her eyes. That brought tears to my eyes. She got up from the bed and sat on the chair next to me. There wasn't room for the two of us. That made it even better. She put her arms around me and hugged me.

As I looked into her eyes, she pulled my head toward her and kissed me. It wasn't a kiss you would see in one of those romantic movies. It wasn't a peck your mother or aunt would give you. It was just a nice kiss. Not only that, but it was also my first kiss, the first time I had ever kissed a girl.

I said, "Wow!"

"Yeah. Wow! I've been waiting for you to kiss me so many times."

"How was I to know?" I asked.

"Boys do develop slower than girls. I guess I've got to teach you everything."

Finally, I asked, "What happens when we get to high school? You'll be a year ahead of me. You'll have all these older friends. You won't want to be seen with a little kid like me."

"Jimmie, you're far from a little kid. No matter what, you'll be my friend."

"You promise?"

She didn't answer. She leaned up and kissed me again. This time, it was a more intimate kiss.

She said, "Those boys in high school, they probably think they're hot stuff. From what I know about those kids, they think way too much of themselves. You don't. You don't think enough of yourself. That's something I've got to change in you."

"Change me? I sort of like the way I am."

"Yes, some things are okay. Some things need help."

"Soon, I'll be going back home. I don't want to," I said.

"It's okay. My mom might let me come stay in town for the rest of the summer."

"That would be nice. It won't be the same. It won't be you and me solving a mystery," I said.

"Yes. We did solve it. Didn't we?" Rachel said.

PART FOUR: JEZEBEL – 1962

CHAPTER 66

HALLOWEEN

I had a plan, and I stuck to it. Everything had gone according to plan. Until it didn't. I had to get away from him, and I would do anything to do so.

First, I had to get out of town. Since I didn't have a car, I had to hitchhike. It was easy for a girl like me to catch a ride. I rode with a kind woman as far as she was going. She dropped me off at the Star Café in New Prague. I bought a Pepsi and slowly drank it, keeping one eye on the door in case my dad followed me and came walking in. After finishing the Pepsi, I walked next door to Tikalsky's Store and bought a new purse and matching wallet, not that I needed one. Because I could. I didn't need his approval anymore.

After an afternoon of hitching a few rides, I made it to Lakeville. I wanted to see Leander. I met him at church camp. He seemed like a nice guy and said he would do anything he could to help me. He said to look for the farm with a Coca-Cola silo on the main road headed east out of town. It didn't take me long before I found it. I was so excited I ran to his farmhouse. I decided to cut through the woods to his house, taking a shortcut. It was a good thing I did because I saw a car pull into the yard. It was my father's car. He had come to find me.

Would I ever be rid of him? I waited in the woods for my father to leave. He didn't leave. He was probably going to wait there until I showed up. I knew him. He was stubborn. It's one thing I knew about him. He was the most stubborn man I have ever known.

There was only one thing to do. I went to see Father Arthur. I told him what he wanted to hear. I told him that I wanted to become a nun. I asked him if he could send me to a convent. This he gladly did after I told him I had the calling.

I think all priests and nuns must believe every person had the calling. Maybe one out of every thousand kids would believe it. I didn't. I needed a place to hide out. I thought a convent would be the safest.

I waited there for a few weeks. While there, I decided to change my appearance. I cut my hair short like the nuns did to convince them I was serious. I hated to lose my beautiful hair, but it was worth it.

I don't think I've ever said so many prayers in all my life. I prayed most to be free of my father and that he wouldn't find me. My mother was no help. I had gone to her, but she thought I was imagining things. She thought my father couldn't be like that even though she had witnessed it many times.

When I had gone to Leander's house, I knew that would be the first place he would look and would continue to search for me. According to Father Arthur, I was right. My father had been all over Lakeville asking anyone if they had seen me. Even pestering some of the girls I had been with at the camp. The only thing left for me was to take Father Arthur's advice to enter the convent.

Life at the convent wasn't too bad, except every day was spent praying. Eventually, I prayed that I wouldn't have to spend another day at the convent. Each day was like the other. Each day I worked and pretended I wanted to be a nun.

I left on Halloween. It would be a perfect time to leave. I would blend in with all the young people out trick or treating. I wouldn't need a costume because I could wear a nun's habit.

I sneaked out of the convent when Mother Superior thought everyone was asleep. Usually, they locked us in. That was another thing that I didn't like. But if I was locked in, it meant my father was locked out.

I feared I might have to protect myself. Before I left the convent, I went into the kitchen, found a butcher knife, and concealed it in my purse. I took a suitcase filled with all my belongings. I would be free to live my life as I wanted.

Shortly after leaving the convent, I noticed a car following me. I was relieved when I saw that it was the mother of a trick or treater making sure her child was safe. The woman who I knew as my mother would never have done that. She probably didn't care that I had never come home. Her life was better without me.

I passed a few more houses and a few more trick or treaters. Some more parents drove by in their cars. I turned the corner onto a dark street. That's when I noticed it. I could never forget this car. It was my dad's car.

How had he found me? He just had a way of doing things like that. He made me get into the car with him. When he turned a corner, I tried to get out of the passenger door. He grabbed my arm and pulled me next to him. He drove with one hand on the wheel and the other on my leg. His fingers lifted the habit. I felt his slimy fingers on my leg. With each mile, his hand inched up my thigh. I kept trying to free myself from his grip. I was no match for him.

He drove out of town and took back country roads. I thought he might be taking me home. Then he stopped on the side of a deserted gravel road. He pulled me even closer to him. His hand moved up my leg. I felt his fingers grope under my panties.

That's when I willed myself to do it. When he wasn't looking, with all my might, I stabbed him under his ribs as hard as I could. Blood came out of his mouth. He sat motionless, so I thought he must be dead. That's when he suddenly reached for me. I pulled the knife out and stuck it into him again. This time he slumped over the steering wheel. I waited, ready to stab him again until I was sure he was dead.

I then had to conceal his body. I drove onto a plowed field. The car bounced up and down as it moved over the furrows. When I was sure a passing driver couldn't see me from the road, I stopped. By moonlight, I dug a hole in the plowed field using the butcher knife. I pulled his body out of the car. I removed his shirt, pants, and boots. I rolled his body into the hole. I then covered the shallow grave with dirt and piled some rocks on top. If a passing motorist had seen me, he would have been surprised to see a nun burying a body in the field!

A farmer would discover his body, but I would be far away. Besides, I had taken all his identification from him. Of course, his wallet contained only a few dollars. I knew he hid some money in the sole of his boot. He didn't believe in banks and didn't want my mom to have anything. I used the butcher knife to cut the soles off his boots. In one of them, I found enough money to get wherever I wanted to go.

I got into the car and drove off the field. When I drove through the ditch, the passenger door flew open, and the boot landed in the ditch. My purse, diary, and wallet slid out of the car and landed in the weeds in the opposite ditch when I fishtailed across the road.

There wasn't time to search through the ditch for anything. I knew it wouldn't be good to be found there and that I needed to get rid of the car. I drove away quickly and hunted until I found a lake with a boat ramp access. I stopped the car short of the shore. My dad kept bottles of whiskey in the car. I opened one, poured the whiskey out, and left the bottle on the floor of the driver's side. I drove the car into the water, jumping out at the last moment.

Then I changed out of the habit into my normal clothes. I sat on the shore and watched as water engulfed the vehicle. They might find the car, but I would be in New York by then.

CHAPTER 67

ADDIE

I wanted to get to New York. First, I had to get to Saint Paul. Once I got there, I would have enough money to catch a bus or a train. Or maybe even fly to New York.

As I walked along in the dark, a car slowed behind me. It was nice to know that it couldn't be my father, but it could have been a policeman or the sheriff. It stopped next to me. A man's voice yelled out from inside the car, asking if I needed a ride. I kept on walking, and soon, he continued on his way. I'd had enough trouble with getting into a car with a man.

Eventually, another car stopped next to me. The driver turned on an interior light. I could see it was a young woman. She rolled down her window and asked if I would like a ride. When I said yes, she asked where I was going. I said I was going to New York. She said she could only take me to New Prague.

It was a start. She told me her name was Gloria. She asked where I was staying. I said I hadn't thought about a place to sleep. She was getting a room at the New Prague Hotel. She was tired and needed to get some sleep. I could stay with her if I wanted.

When we walked into the New Prague Hotel, a woman named Addie was behind the counter. Only one room was available, with one bed and a pull-out couch.

After we got to the room, I unfolded the couch, dropped onto the mattress without undressing, and fell asleep almost immediately. I didn't know killing someone could take so much out of a person.

I woke up in the morning to a quiet room. I looked over to the bed and saw that Gloria had already gotten up. I went down to look for her in the restaurant. Not finding her there, I went to the front desk and asked Addie if she had seen Gloria. She told me Gloria had left before the sun came up.

I went back up to the room and checked my belongings. My bag was there, but all my money was gone. The money I was going to use to get to New York.

I met Addie as I went down the stairs. She asked me who was going to pay for the room. I had assumed Gloria had. Addie told me I had two options. One was to pay her. The other was to call the police. I didn't want the police involved. I suggested a third option, working it off. She said she always needed help, so she put me to work in the restaurant for two weeks.

It was a nice enough job. Men that worked for Robin Hood Flour ate breakfast and lunch there. Workers from Kratchovil Construction, Minnesota Valley Breeders, and the feed mills stopped in for meals too. Even some of the merchants in town met for coffee.

The only trouble was that Addie was a slave driver. She worked me so hard that I thought she would make a great Mother Superior at the convent. The only thing missing was the prayers. However, I prayed that I would soon be free of Addie.

She worked her son, Scott, hard too. He had no way of escaping. I did. That happened after the second week. Addie offered me a permanent job. Even though I liked the job and the people, there was one problem. Addie would be my boss.

CHAPTER 68

THAT DARN PURSE

I grabbed my things and walked down the street. I wanted to go to New York, but I didn't have enough money. I did have enough to buy a hamburger and fries at Frank's Drive-In. When I asked Frank if he was hiring, he told me he ran the place himself. There were no jobs at the Ben Franklin Five & Dime and Gambles Hardware Store.

Up ahead, I saw Tikalsky's Store, a place I remembered. The place where I bought the purse. I saw a "help wanted" sign in the window.

I got the job at Tikalsky's, stocking shelves and running the cash register. When they hired me, I asked if they might know of a place to stay. They gave me a room upstairs for free. It was mainly a storage closet with a window to the alley. It had a bed which was all I needed.

I started working there just before Thanksgiving. I saved my money, not bothering to eat anything for days. I even picked up extra money working for Addie, helping serve the breakfast crowd. I was able to put up with her for a couple of hours a day.

One morning the next June, when I was working in the back room, I heard Clara talking to a young couple. They asked about me. Clara hadn't recognized me. How could she? I had shorter hair now, and it had been so long ago.

It was through my purse that two young kids had traced me here. I had tried to find that purse before but had no idea exactly where to look. They were lucky enough to find it. Unlucky for me. Clara told them I had been headed to Shakopee. That would keep them busy. I wondered how long it would take to trace me back here.

After they left, I found out from Clara where the young girl was living. That's when I decided to keep those two from looking for me. I went to the farm several times and left letters in the mailbox, telling them to stop looking for me. I never would have hurt his dog, but I didn't want them to get too close. I hoped they would get the hint. They didn't.

I decided to call Leander. He was surprised to hear from me. He had heard I had left the convent but hadn't told anyone. He told me the young couple had been there looking for me. That's when I decided I needed to leave town.

One morning, in the middle of June, I packed up my things. I stopped at the hotel to pick up my last paycheck. Addie wasn't there. She had gone to Saint Paul on business. If I had known, I might have gotten a ride with her. Her son, Shep, no relation to Jimmie's dog, paid me in cash. I left New Prague and took a bus to Saint Paul. My last stop would be New York City. The city of opportunity. The place where I wanted to go. A place where I would be safe in a city of nine million people. I didn't know anyone in New York. That was a good thing.

PART FIVE: JANA - 1876

CHAPTER 69

BAD TO WORSE

I walked out of the cave into the blizzard. The snow seemed to come down harder with each step. I had to clear my mind. I'd felt sorry for myself long enough. Hiding in the cave didn't help.

I wandered around the woods for I don't know how long. I came to a lake I had never seen before. I walked around it to the other side and sat on an old stump. I thought about my life with Vojta. He was a good man. At first, maybe not. Toward the end, he realized that I was perfect for him. He needed someone like me. I lost our baby, but we could have another son.

I decided right then that I would change. My attitude would improve. I would go back to Vojta, and it would be like it was before. Next year, we would have a cabin and we would start a family.

I decided to cut across the lake this time because I was anxious to get back. About twenty yards from the shoreline, the ice cracked. I could hear it below the snow. I turned to run back, but it was too late. Within seconds, I fell through the ice and into the freezing water.

I tried to get back on the ice, trying to find a hold. However, I kept falling back in. After about the third or fourth time, I realized I couldn't get out of the water.

Someone from the shore called out to me. He told me to hang on. Hang on to what, I wondered. As I struggled to stay above water, I knew I couldn't last much longer. Then my world went black.

CHAPTER 70

OUT OF MY MIND

When I next opened my eyes, I found myself in a strange bed. I tried to get up, but I had no energy. I soon fell back asleep. I was awakened constantly by fits of coughs which hurt my chest.

A man and woman stood at the side of the bed. They said their names were George and Ruth. Ruth told George that I probably caught pneumonia and that I needed a doctor. He left and came back later without a doctor but with some pills.

I asked to go home, to go back to my cave. When they heard that, they both thought I was delirious and that I didn't know what I was talking about. I insisted that I lived in a cave.

They just shook their heads and made me take a pill. They said it would help me sleep. I don't know how long I slept. Every time I woke up, they made me take another pill which made me fall asleep again.

I finally started to get some strength back. The cold in my chest cleared up. Ruth told me to eat, that I hadn't eaten much in the whole month. I had been there for a whole month! It seemed like only a few days. I felt weak and needed food to regain my strength.

That was one thing I could do quite well. At first, they fed me only soup. After one cup, I felt like I had over-eaten. Gradually, I had portions of bread and potatoes.

When I was strong enough to leave, they resisted. They thought I was still crazy from the fever and was hallucinating about living in a cave. There was no way I could convince them, so I spoke no more about it.

After about a week, I was up and about helping them with their chores around the house. They decided it was safe for me to travel and packed up some food. I saw something off to the side that I wanted and asked if I could take it along. They said I was welcome to it.

Before I left, I asked them how I could repay them. George warned me not to wander out onto the middle of the lake in a blizzard. He didn't think he had it in him to save anyone again.

CHAPTER 71
LOST WITHOUT ME

When I got back, I expected to find Vojta waiting for me. There was no sign of him. Perhaps, he was out hunting. A lot of good that would do. Without me, he was probably starving by now. Maybe he was out looking for me. That's something he would do. He would never give up on me.

I searched through the cave and found the walls I was looking for. I then took out the can of paint George and Ruth had given me. I began to paint my farm scene along the walls of the cave. I found another thing that I wasn't good at. However, it did sort of look like a farmyard.

After I finished painting the wall, I checked to see if Vojta had returned. His chair was empty. I sat down and noticed his journal on the table next to me. Many times I'd seen him writing in it but I'd never read it before. I thought he might have wanted to keep that private. I couldn't stop myself. I picked up the journal and started reading. I was amazed at everything we had done. Some things I had forgotten.

When I got to the last chapter, I saw he hadn't given up on me. He had searched for me the entire time I had been gone, just in the wrong places. I was surprised to find out he had left for New York City to find me.

There was only one thing to do. I packed up some of my things. There wasn't room for everything in my bag. I hated to leave the books. It was

LYING IN THE WEEDS

spring and the weather had started to clear a bit. It would make my trip a little easier.

I didn't know what I was going to do for money since I didn't have a penny to my name. I knew that I had to search for Vojta. Fortunately, Marek gave me what little he had, so I could get part of the way.

If Vojta was looking for me in New York, I would have to try to find him. He would be helpless without me. He needed me by his side, and I knew one day I would be. All I had to do was find him in New York. How hard could that be?

THE END

ACKNOWLEDGEMENTS

A special thanks to my writers' group in Minnesota, the Writers' Rung, and to my writers' group in Florida, the Fiction Writers' Group of Tarpon Springs for their tremendous support and feedback. I would like to thank Ben Bartusek, Dr. Thomas Kajer, and George Mikiska for Czech immigration history from the 19th Century and Daniel Shepard for his tireless proofreading.

Cover photography by Curt Tilleraas

Made in the USA
Monee, IL
27 July 2023

40007504R00154